THE AQUARIA CHRONICLES

MELANIE DIXON

THE AQUARIA CHRONICLES
**Book One: Aqua Marine; Book Two: Aqua Marine
Biologist; Book Three: Aqua Mariner;
Book Four: The Cure**

ISBN: 9781366269768

Cover & Interior Design by Melanie Dixon

Dixon, Melanie
The Aquaria Chronicles / Melanie Dixon.–2nd ed.
Visit the author: https://meldawn.wixsite.com/
melaniedawndixon

DEDICATION

The Aquaria Chronicles

I'd like to thank Isabel, who has
always purred for me the past ten years.

TABLE OF CONTENTS

The Aquaria Chronicles

TABLE OF CONTENTS

The Aquaria Chronicles

BOOK ONE—AQUA MARINE

The Aquaria Chronicles

PROLOGUE

The Aquaria Chronicles

I WAS AT THE UNIVERSITY OF BRITISH COLUMBIA registration desk paying my fees when the alarm sounded.

"What is that?" I asked, looking around me worriedly.

"Probably another bleed infestation," the admittance clerk replied.

"Are we done then? I should probably be getting back home," I asked.

"Yes, we are done," she said.

I pulled my respirator from my bag and started turning towards the door.

"Oh, and one more thing," she called out to me.

"Yes?" I asked, irritated to get to safety before it was too late.

"There are no refunds in the event the course is cancelled."

"Why would there be no refunds? I paid my money, surely it wouldn't be my fault if classes were cancelled?"

The clerk pushed her glasses up her nose. "Well, to put it delicately, there may be no university to come to by the fall." The clerk jerked her head in the direction of the window.

Outside, a fine powdery layer of blue floated to the ground. I watched as it covered the face of one man. He fell to the ground, clutching his neck, while his entire face turned blue. Soon, he stopped moving.

CHAPTER ONE—PERCOLATE

The Aquaria Chronicles

I GRABBED MY DENIM JACKET for the cool Vancouver summer air, and was gently nudging the front door open when I heard stomping noises come up behind me.

"Aqua. Just where do you think you're going?" my mother called out to me.

"Where do you think I'm going? I've only been talking about Japan Dolphins Day for the past six months!"

She shoved in front of me and slammed the door shut. I do believe that I was in trouble now.

"Put your jacket and keys away. That is a protest. Lord knows what will happen there. You could be tossed in the slammer or worse, injured."

"Or, the dolphins could even be saved!" I slapped my jacket back on the peg and tossed my keys on the table. There was no point in keeping them. She would take them from me, to keep me from driving to Vancouver where the Japanese Consulate was located.

We lived in a heritage house in Queen's Park, New Westminster. While the area was prestigious, our house was modest. My mum, Helen Marsden, had bought it with the money she had earned as a registered nurse.

I think she was feeling a bit guilty, as she sidled up to me to give me a hug. I hugged back a little.

"Why don't I make you some lemonade and popcorn and you can watch the protest on TV?"

"Sure Mum. That's great." What else could I say?

Her arm dropped from my shoulder.

"However, I expect you to give the jacuzzi a good scrubbing later. I want it sparkling clean. There is bleed all over it."

Of course there were strings attached but I smiled warmly anyway. She wasn't a bad mother but she couldn't accept that I was seventeen years old and nearly an adult.

The jacuzzi cleaning would be quite a chore. Over the past several months this awful weed had sprung up in New West. We called it "bleed" as it was a deep blue colour. It was as nasty as touching poison ivy or oak, and when it dried out it turned into a fine dust which caused allergic reactions. It was quite toxic to asthmatics. I'd have to be kitted out before I could touch it.

I wasn't going to whine and complain too much as I had some news for my mother later, and she wasn't going to like it.

Mirabel snuggled with me on my lap. She was the tabby I had rescued from Katie's Place animal shelter in Maple Ridge. They were actually a no-kill shelter, but I gave her a good home in a real house rather than sharing with 200 other cats.

I switched to the news. I hoped there would be mention of International Dolphins Day. Dolphins Day was founded by Ric O'Barry and the SJD—Save Japan Dolphins—to bring awareness to the plight of these beautiful sea creatures from the Taiji Bay in Japan.

Back in 2009, The Cove documentary won an Academy award, and first brought international awareness to the dolphin cull each year. Once a year, thousands of people show up at Japanese Consulates around the world to peacefully lend their support in helping Japan to stop killing these intelligent mammals.

The beginning of the news mentioned nothing of the protest. There was still a full hour to go though, so I wasn't too concerned. The yearly protest was still building steam.

The news anchor started off with today's bleed levels. Was it safe to go outside, was it a good day to stay at home, or was it a day that people had to enter their bunkers? While the bleed thrived in the mild climate of the Lower Mainland, it dried up pretty fast if it wasn't raining. If it were a particularly windy day it could wreck havoc on the city. There were Special Forces who did nothing but keep it under control. So far it had not spread beyond the Lower Mainland. It stayed away from the U.S.A., northern B.C. and the Okanagan regions.

Today, apparently it was a good day to go outside.

That meant a good day for a protest. I was getting a bit bored with the news so took some time to pet Mirabel. She was a very needy cat. I was happy to make her purr hungrily for more lovin's.

My Mum walked in and put a huge bowl of popcorn on the couch, plus a large glass of lemonade on the coffee table. I was hoping she'd stay but she took off again.

Mirabel purred contentedly. We watched the news until it was nearly seven o'clock. Finally, a scene popped up of hundreds of people surrounding the Japanese Consulate in downtown Vancouver.

"Hey Mum, come and watch this," I cried out to her.

She popped into the room and sat beside me. We nibbled on popcorn. We watched as one of the reporters lifted a microphone to his mouth.

"Hi, I'm Sandeep Singh. Today is August 30, 2018. I'm standing in front of the Japanese Consulate building where hundreds are gathered to protest the annual slaughter of dolphins in Taiji, Japan." The reporter stood in front of the steps of the building. A short clip was played, showing the carnage in the Bay. Soon, its waters were coloured red.

I could not watch. I covered my eyes.

"It's just a little blood Aqua. What do you think happens to the animals we eat?" my mother said to me.

"Well, I'll become a vegetarian then. Who says

humans have the right to treat animals this way?" I was getting agitated so Mirabel leaped off the couch and sidled out of the room.

"You do have a point dear but things aren't changing any time soon. The documentary won an award nine years ago, but has the killing stopped?" She waved her hand at the TV.

I replied back, "It's all about bringing awareness to the issue. A change isn't going to happen overnight. Perhaps one day this will be a thing of the past."

Mum looked like she was getting bored with the news. The scene had switched back to some of the protesters being interviewed.

"I don't know why you have this great interest in fish," Mum said, her forehead creasing with frown lines.

"Mum, dolphins are mammals, like us. They're highly intelligent, some say as much as humans are." I felt a bit irritated by her attitude. Well, since I was already agitated, this was as good a time as any to bring up my news.

"Mum, I have something to tell you," I said, gently touching her arm.

"Can't it wait? I need to get ready for my shift at the hospital." She stood up and exited the living room.

"Not really. University is starting next week," I said, raising my voice.

"Oh, it's about school." She came back into the living room and sat beside me again. "I'm so excited you earned your bachelor's of science, and are heading on your way to your first year of medical school."

I shook my head in the negative. She was going to be upset.

"That's just it, Mum. I wanted to talk to you about it."

She had a concerned look on her face. "It will be tough, but you're smart, you can do it. If I'd had the resources I could have been a doctor too."

How was I going to break the news to her? She wanted her only child to become a medical doctor, a chance she never had.

"I'm really sorry Mum. I'm not going to medical school." I looked away from her.

My Mum, who was almost constantly in nervous motion, came to a dead stop.

"You're not going back to school?" She started getting mad. "Just what will you do? Do you want a break before going back to school?"

"No breaks. I am going back to school next week. I just won't be attending medical school."

"Aqua, we discussed this. You applied at medical school and were accepted. I paid the tuition, and now you are going!"

"No Mum, I changed my major," I said, looking back at her.

She stood up and hovered over me. "This is ridiculous. I paid for medical school, because I never had the chance. My parents couldn't afford to send me, so I had to attend nursing school instead, while they sent my brother to medical school in my rightful place!"

"I understand that Mum. I'm still going to be a doctor, just not for humans." I stood up beside her.

"What do you mean, not for humans?" she asked, her eyes widening.

"I'm going to become a marine biologist." By this point I was standing beside her, the protest on the TV forgotten.

"That is ridiculous." She slapped her hands against her waist so it made her look bigger, and quite intimidating.

"Did you forget you named me Aqua? Get it, Aqua. Water. Aqua?" I said back at her.

"Your father named you. And that is just a name." She swung both of her arms out. She never hit me, but I think she might have come close, just this one time.

"It's my name and it's appropriate," I said.

"A vet? You want to become a fish vet? How useless is that? I can't believe you went behind my back, used my hard-earned dollars and changed your major. You can forget having me paying even a dime to your schooling again. I am done!"

With that she stormed out of the room. I grabbed the bowl of popcorn and flung it against the TV really hard. Nothing happened to it, except for a bit of grease oozing slowly down the screen.

Well, it was a good thing that my first year of marine biology was paid for, but once the year was up, I was going to have to find another way to finance my education. I supposed I could take a job at the Vancouver Aquarium. I was there every weekend and they had already offered it to me. I had originally been focussed on studying, but now a part-time job seemed like a good idea.

I heard my Mum leave the house a short time later to go to her job at the hospital. She could still become a doctor; I'm not sure what her problem was. I'd heard about registered nurses entering medical school to complete their doctorate degrees.

Since I was already in the dog house I decided I'd better not antagonize her further. It was time to hunker down and clean out the jacuzzi.

I had to fully suit up in what appeared to be a biohazard suit. This one was made especially for clearing out bleed. I was covered head-to-toe in white flexible plastic, complete with astronaut's helmet, rubber gloves, and breathing apparatus.

Not every family had one of these, but since we were in the affluent area, most of us had our own suits. It was either that or let the Force come onto our property once a week to do damage control. Most in my area tended to clear out the bleed themselves. It afforded great privacy, though the inspectors came once a month to have a look around. Anyone caught with more than a ten centimetre square patch of bleed was fined. That patch could grow into a metre wide overnight.

I drained the jacuzzi first then scrubbed all the blue and white tiles surrounding the gazebo. The bleed tended to congregate on the ground, rather in the air, so it didn't take me long to set up the ladder and do a full sweep of the gazebo roof and beams.

Mirabel wandered around the garden while I did this. For some reason, the bleed didn't affect animals, only humans. At least I'd never heard of any related animal deaths, but thousands of humans had succumbed.

Which was why it was so important that I suited up and scrubbed the area clean. Bleed was neutralized by simple water, though I liked to add a bit of dish soap. Might as way actually clean the area too.

Once everything was sparkling clean, I decontaminated myself by hosing myself off before putting the suit away.

I think by now I was exhausted. I had been thwarted by attending a protest that was dear to my heart. My friends were probably wondering where I was. Watching it on TV had been okay, but the confrontation with my Mum left me feeling emotionally drained.

Was I right in pursuing my own happiness? Ever since I had been a kid I wanted to work with animals.

At first I thought I'd be a vet, then after a few trips to the aquarium I realized that I wanted to be a marine biologist.

I'd gone behind my Mum's back and switched my university application. I'd known she would flip out when she heard I did not really want to be a medical doctor. She should understand though. She hadn't really gone to school for what she wanted to be either. So why couldn't she understand my true passion was marine life? Plus, the tuition fees were a lot less money for this field. She would eventually be grateful that I had saved her cash in the long run, right?

The jacuzzi filled with water. It took a while for the heaters to raise the water to a respectable temperature. I should really call my friend Heather, my closest friend, and let her know what had happened. I'm something of a loner, so I only have a few close friends. But I'd see her tomorrow at the Aquarium. She'd be excited I was going to accept the job, plus I could tell her all about my pathetic little day.

I stripped down and hopped into the jacuzzi. I placed a towel behind my neck. The warm water bubbled around me. The day wasn't too hot and the water wasn't quite heated enough, but I began to relax.

I was just starting to nod off. I dreamed of a world encompassed by the blue weed, suffocating all human life, leaving a blanket of softness for the animals to sleep on. I felt a wet ball of fur land on my chest. I opened my eyes and lifted my head.

Mirabel. She had jumped into the water and was on my chest, kneading my skin with her paws. Her finely pointed claws tips would occasionally brush my skin.

I didn't mind the kneading but I was a bit worried she might figure out what she had done and I'd be ripped to shreds as a result.

"Umm, Mirabel, do you really want to be here?" She gazed at me with her wide open yellow eyes and purred. She made me smile. I'd adopted her right after my Dad had died. She saved my life. I loved her so much, even more than my mother.

She carefully plodded up my chest and crawled to the edge of the jacuzzi. She lay down on the towel beside my head.

I reached out a hand to pat her. She didn't seem to mind the water. She'd never done anything like this before. We both had a nice rest that evening. It was a great way to let my cares ease away as I mused over the day.

CHAPTER TWO—ACTIVATE

The Aquaria Chronicles

HEATHER WAS TAKING ME ON A WHIRLWIND TOUR of behind-the-scenes aquarium life. We were viewing sections that were off-limits to tourists—these were for employees-only. They set the stage for the shows and events of the Vancouver Aquarium. I'd filled out the new employee paperwork, been accepted, and was now working my first day of paid work.

I'd volunteered my time at the Aquarium before, but this was the first time I was actually working to full capacity as an official employee. There hadn't been a lot of time for me to chat about private stuff with my best friend Heather, who was a supervisor at the Penguin Point exhibit. We'd spent most of the morning in a meeting with our boss Stephen. He'd given me the rundown on rules, regulations and safety at the Aquarium. I had been given a two-hundred page handbook to read at home.

"So now that I've met the head honcho and he is back in his office, I can tell you about what happened yesterday afternoon," I said to Heather. We were now on the tourist side of the Aquarium.

"Do tell. Last I heard, you were going to tell your

Mum that you were dropping out of med school to pursue a highly rewarding career as a marine biologist."

"That's right. I broke the news to her last night."

Heather stopped wiping down the railing surrounding the penguin habitat. "Your Mum is pretty cool. Did she take the news well?"

I threw my hands up in the air. "Hell no, she flipped out. Can you believe it?"

One of the penguins walked up to the edge of the enclosure. Heather made cooing noises before turning her attention back to me.

"No way! I thought she'd understand. She seems like a smart enough lady."

"No, unfortunately not. She made me feel guilty, as I have the opportunity that she never did. Her Dad sent her to nursing school, not med school. Only the boys in the family got to go to medical school. She had her heart set on me attending."

"Oh great. She could still go. She must make enough money to go back to school," Heather suggested. She pushed a lock of blonde hair back behind her ear.

"Well, I know that, you know that, my cat knows that, but she can't figure it out for herself. I'm so annoyed." I scratched my head. There was a small bit of wind picking up.

It appeared that Heather had a new boyfriend. The penguin was right at the edge of the habitat, trying to jump up and attract her attention. He was a cute little guy—he couldn't have been more than six months old. Heather was oblivious to him.

"I'm sure she'll come around." Heather gave me a little hug, which I accepted willingly. "Parents! They think they know what is best for us, but they really don't." She shook her head.

I took the rag from her and continued polishing the railing.

"I know. I can't believe the big guilt trip she laid on me. I'm sorry she didn't become a physician in her field, but it's really not too late. And get this, she told me that she won't pay a penny more for my education if I pursue a career in marine biology. I'll have to finance it myself. I have a bit of savings but not enough for a second full year of marine biology."

Heather looked sympathetic. "That's awful. No wonder you accepted my standing job offer. You're going to need every penny for next year."

"Am I ever. At least I don't have to worry about this year, as I switched my application to marine biology without her approval."

"Really? That's crazy. You must be growing up if you're starting to think for yourself." Heather wore a suitably impressed expression upon her face.

I slapped her on the shoulder. "Don't you know it! It's time we flew the coop."

We giggled together.

She added, "We'll fly the coop once the next two years are up. We should be able to find a pretty decent job with a Masters Degree, then we can work our way towards a doctorate. Perhaps we can share our first apartment together until we make the big bucks."

I smiled and she picked up the bucket and mop while I followed her back to HQ. We were both taking the same program at UBC–University of British Columbia. We had initially met each other at the Aquarium about four years ago, and had quickly became best friends since then.

We were sipping hot tea and having crumpets in the break room, near the cafe, when a tourist came barging into our office. A wave of irritation flew through me. I was just starting to relax after the stress of yesterday, plus coping with my new job took me down a notch.

The short, balding man wildly waved his arms around. "Do either of you ladies know CPR? A boy has collapsed on the ground outside."

I responded, "I do, I have Level Three First Aid." I looked worriedly at Heather.

"You go, I'll call an ambulance." She went to find her purse which had her cell phone in it.

After I grabbed our first aid kit from the holder on the wall, the man and I raced off towards the penguin exhibit.

A small boy lay on the ground near the penguin

enclosure. He was motionless. A thin veil of bleed covered every exposed surface of his skin. I pushed open the first aid kit and grabbed the bottle of spray antiseptic and some gauze. I sprayed his face and wiped off the bleed.

"Is this your son?" I asked the man.

"No, I don't know where his parents are. I found him lying here a few minutes ago."

I checked to see if he was breathing and detected a small amount of air coming from his nostrils. Since a bleed poisoning almost always involved an allergic reaction, I sifted through my kit until I found a bottle of liquid Benadryl. Being a Level Three First Aid Attendant meant I was qualified to administer basic medicines. I poured a tiny amount of Benadryl into his mouth.

"Can you find a supervisor and tell them there is bleed all over the place? This is not good, the weather has turned quickly." I had a quick look around. Surely this had not been here when Heather and I had cleaned up the penguin enclosure an hour ago?

"I'm on it," he yelled as he took off towards the main building.

I checked the boy's vital signs. His breathing had improved, and his pulse was speeding up. I shifted him over into recovery position. He was about six years old. Where on earth were his parents? Surely they wouldn't leave a six-year-old to wander the aquarium on his own, unless accompanied by a guide?

The man hadn't returned yet. There was no sign of Heather. A soft cloud of bleed was settling down on the ground. Where was it coming from? The day was a bit windy. It must be growing in a patch somewhere. The wind must have loosened and blown it through the air.

I pulled off my hoodie and placed it over the boy's head. He didn't need to breathe in any more of that crap.

I yanked my dolphin t-shirt over my nose and mouth. I didn't need to breathe any in either, though so far I hadn't had any allergic reactions since we had been plagued with this junk. I checked on the boy every few seconds, while gazing madly around. Where were his…?

I had a sickening feeling as I gazed into the penguin habitat. The penguins were quite agitated and all congregated at the far side of the enclosure. Right below I could see a mass of green cloth.

A hand grabbed me from behind. "Get indoors now! It's not safe out here." It was Stephen dressed in a biohazard suit. He pushed me towards the building. I ran ahead while Stephen grabbed the boy in his arms. Heather was beckoning us to rush, holding the door open. We rushed through and she slammed it closed behind us. Any tourists seated were told to stand near the wall.

Stephen placed the boy on one of the tables. I

checked and he seemed to be doing well. He was stirring a bit and coughing. I opened his mouth but saw no sign of the dreaded bleed.

"I think he'll be okay," I said.

"The ambulance is on the way," Heather announced.

Stephen yelled, "I'm going back out there to get his parents!"

"Please be careful Stephen," Heather called. He was a great guy—neither of us wanted anything to happen to him. Hopefully he had the right level biohazard suit. There were three levels, just like the three degrees of bleed that could be outside at any given time.

We heard sirens and moved some chairs and tables out of the way to make room for the parents. The paramedics came storming in with their cases and took care of the boy.

Stephen came in with the mother. She was in bad shape and coughing up blood. She must have breathed in a large amount of the weed, but she was lucky as they had gotten to her in time.

I was waiting for Stephen to leave again to grab the father, but he shook his head at me. He went to speak to the paramedics.

A tear slid down my cheek. What was happening with our world? Where had this horrendous blue weed come from that suffocated its victims until they died?

Why did we have a bad fall today when yesterday had been fine? Heather and I hugged each other. There didn't seem much else we could do.

Stephen came up to us. "The boy will be fine, and they'll rush the mother to the hospital. With luck, she'll make it too. Sadly, the father didn't make it. I found him covering her—he saved her life. I want both of you to go home now. There is a level two warning in effect, due to wind. It's starting to rain now, so it should be safe enough to get home." His cell phone rang then and interrupted him.

Heather and I grabbed our belongings.

"I really think you should come with me Aqua. If it gets worse we can hole up in my North Vancouver bunker, which is awesome. We even have individual rooms, and a separate bathroom."

"I'd accept your offer—you know I want us to stay together, but I have to connect with my Mum, and get my cat. I can't leave Mirabel alone in the house. Who knows how long we'll need to stay underground." I gave her my regrets.

"I'm sad to hear this." Her little mouth turned under. "I'll give you a lift to the Skytrain. I'm sorry I can't drive you further, but this sounds like a level two infestation, and I have to head to North Van when that happens."

A level two infestation meant we had to hole up for a bit in our bunkers.

"Please, don't worry about it. I promised my Mum I'd head for home at any sign of trouble. We haven't had an infestation like this for months," I said to her.

"A patch must have snuck in behind some bushes and reproduced."

"God, I hate this stuff," I replied.

"Let's get out of here while we can." Heather grabbed the last of her belongings off the table.

We were heading out the door when Stephen came back to us.

"Bad news. The force are recommending we hole up in our bunkers until it gets rained out. I think you ladies have about an hour to get home."

We grabbed some face masks from the emergency kit. Waving bye-bye rapidly, we ran for Heather's car. I didn't see any bleed, but that was no guarantee that it wasn't out there.

Heather drove quickly but carefully to the Skytrain station. It seemed like the traffic was worse this afternoon. I guess everyone was going home. The bleed was like a bad snowfall—everyone headed for home until it dissipated.

"Do you have a cell phone yet?" she asked me, before I opened the door to get out at Burrard Station.

"No, my Mum won't let me have one. She said it'll take valuable time away from my studies."

"That sucks. Here, take mine. I can use my sister's and call you later."

I grabbed it from her. "Do we really have to go to the bunkers?" I dreaded the thought of being cooped up in a tiny room with my Mum for a day.

"Don't know. I'm sure we'll figure it out when we get home. Have a nice evening."

"Good bye," I said, shutting the door behind me.

The Skytrain station was packed. Lots of people took transit from downtown Vancouver. It was definitely the green way of travelling. Parking rates were also through the roof, particularly if you needed to be there all day. Vancouver had a great Skytrain transit system. Unfortunately, once I reached Columbia Station in New Westminster, I couldn't say the same for the bus system. I had no choice but to stand in a bus shelter and wait for a bus that would take its time getting to me.

There was bleed floating lazily through the air. Today was definitely a bunker day. We had these little bunkers built into the centres of our homes. They came equipped with a built-in filtration system, plus plenty of food and water to last for a week or two. That was long enough for it to start raining again. It rained at least once a week in the Lower Mainland.

The cell phone rang.

"Are you home yet?" Heather asked breathlessly, without even waiting for me to say hi.

"Nope. I'm crammed into a bus shelter with twenty other people. I should be home in about ten minutes."

"Maybe you should call your mother to let her know you are coming?"

"Good idea. Are you at home?"

"Yes, I am. Once we go into the shelter there will be too much cell phone interference."

"Well, take it easy. I'll call you when I can," I said to her.

We said our goodbyes. The bus came then, so I forgot to call my Mum. It was a short five minutes up the hill. I adjusted my face mask then ran out the back doors to head for home.

CHAPTER THREE—WAIT

The Aquaria Chronicles

I RACED UP THE HILL TO MY HOUSE. When I reached the back of the house I stripped off my clothes and hosed myself down thoroughly. The cold water was shocking but I was sweaty and gritty from the bleed, so I was grateful to finally get it off me. I was fully expecting my Mum to be there with a warm towel but she didn't come out. Perhaps she was waiting for me inside the bunker.

I left my clothes outside. I could deal with them at a later date, but I kept my purse with me. I entered the house and headed to the bathroom to towel off. I thought it odd that Mirabel didn't run in to greet me. If my Mum was already in the bunker perhaps she took my cat in too.

I went to my room and there was still no sign of my cat. I got dressed and found my duffel bag.

"Here kitty kitty," I called.

I filled up my duffel bag with what I thought I might need for the week, plus a book or two. Still no sign of my cat.

Giving up, I headed for the bunker, which was actually a closet located in the middle of the hallway. I pulled open the door. We didn't keep it locked. There was no point, as bleed couldn't unlock doors. Inside were two transparent aluminum doors. They were like clear glass, but much stronger. I pressed a button on the middle of one of the doors and it slid soundlessly open. Once open the inner lights turned on. No, there was no one inside the six foot by four foot space. That was odd. My Mum wouldn't be at the hospital for her shift for a few hours yet, so where was she?

Perhaps she had gone shopping and got stuck at the mall? I really shouldn't be concerned, she could look after herself. There were safe shelters all over the place. And perhaps the cat was outside. She'd be fine out there, if need be, but I'd better make sure before I locked myself in the shelter.

I took a tour around the house, looking for some sign of the cat, or even a note from my mother. Mirabel did not answer to the can opener in the kitchen, nor to me shaking a bag of her crunchies. I tossed them in the duffel bag I had slung over my shoulder just in case I found her. I was starting to get really worried. This was the cat I'd had for the past nine years. The cat that had gotten me through my father's death.

My Dad had died of prostate cancer when I little. I should have been too young to understand what was happening, but I had found my mother's medical texts and looked up "prostate cancer".

By the time he'd found out he had cancer he had only months left to live. I was extremely traumatized by the whole process. The endless chemo treatments, trips to the hospital, and watching him throw up in the bathroom afterwards. To no avail, he died anyway. One day I awoke to sobbing coming from my parent's room and I knew he had passed away. I took his death so hard that all Mum could do was look after me, so she had hidden much of her grieving to keep me going. She was one tough lady.

Then one day, after I had been moping around the house for way too long, she had announced we were going on a special trip. She drove me out to this special animal shelter called "Katie's Place" in Maple Ridge. Katie had been the founding cat and this animal shelter now housed nearly 200 cats. It was their forever home, should no one ever adopt them. I played with the cats all day long, but none immediately stood out to me. And then I saw her sitting on a tall scratching post in the back. She gazed at me and I gazed back. It was love at first sight. We adopted her and I've loved her ever since.

There was nothing left for me to do but check outside for the cat and then go and hole up in the bunker for a day or so. The bleed was contaminating the air and it was best to stay indoors. I could be upset about my cat missing, or I could look for her to the best of my abilities, and carry on if I didn't find her.

I had no sooner opened the door when she rushed through the small opening. I had been a bit wary, not wishing to let in any of the bleed.

"Mirabel! You naughty girl. Where were you? I was so worried. How could you do this to me?" I scolded her but she gazed up at me and purred. She wanted to snuggle, but she was covered in the bleed. I'd have to give her a bath. She was going to be thrilled at me for that. She had joined me in the jacuzzi, but that had been on her own terms, and no soap or scrubbing had been involved.

I donned some rubber gloves and picked her up and placed her in the kitchen sink. She gave me a look that said, "How dare you do this to me!"

"Easy girl, the sooner we wash this off you, the better."

I plugged the drain and filled the sink with hot water. I squeezed in a tiny bit of dish soap. Perhaps the bubbles would distract her?

She cried as I scrubbed her clean. She was a sweet kitty—she never tried to bite or claw me. I cleaned her as quickly as possible, then pulled the plug. I rinsed her under the tap. She growled at me, but did nothing. She tolerated water on her own terms, like the day she had jumped into the jacuzzi with me.

I grabbed a few dishcloths and proceeded to dry her. She turned her head and licked her neck.

"Good girl, what a good kitty you are."

Mirabel started howling. This was odd. She should have howled while I washed her, not when it was nearly over.

I saw something flash past my eyes. I let Mirabel jump off the counter while I looked up.

Outside, the backyard was covered in a film of blue powder. Bleed covered the bushes and trees. It covered the gazebo. So much for clearing it yesterday. It fell slowly and steadily from the air, like snow. It could be neutralized on the ground, but since it was so light, it had a habit of floating back up into the air and moving into another yard. And then I heard the emergency sirens go off. These were the sirens that the city had for times of emergency, to go along with that emergency broadcast channel. It was time to pack up and head into the bunker.

I found the cat carrier and placed Mirabel inside. I grabbed both my purse, and my duffel bag. I hoped the window seals would hold until I could reach the hallway.

There was no need to worry, and the bunker was already open. I placed the carrier and the bags inside, then stepped in. I closed the door. The bunker was really an extra precaution, but most homes were double sealed at windows and doors to keep the fine dust of the blue weed out.

I pressed the button on the invisible aluminum doors and they silently slid shut. We were now holed up in our shelter for who knew how long. I only recalled one other infestation like this before, about six months ago.

It was going to be a long wait but we both had cat food and human food, water, blankets and a pullout bed. There were books and cable TV, but the cell phone reception likely wouldn't work in here.

I wondered how Heather and her family were faring. They had a larger bunker than we did, as they were part of a larger family. I briefly wished I had just gone home with her but then I would have worried endlessly about my cat.

I decided to give the phone a try anyway. I pressed the button to turn on the cell phone. NO SERVICE blazed on its small screen. Great. Why didn't these bunkers have a built-in telephone? If there was ever an emergency within the bunker, we were left to our own devices.

I decided to unpack my supplies instead. There were several cupboards built into the furthest wall. Many contained supplies, but I found one that was empty. I emptied the contents of my duffel bag and put my purse inside a cupboard. Once that stuff was out of the way I was able to open up the cat carrier and let Mirabel out.

She had been polite about the whole process but she looked relieved to be out. I had to stow the carrier in one corner as there was no way it was going to fit in any of the remaining cabinets. This shelter was built tiny. Perhaps it was a good thing my Mum had found another place to stay.

Speaking of her, I imagined that by now she was worried about me. But she must be thinking that I was still at work, likely holed up in the bunker there. She would have had no idea that we had been sent home. I'm sure her mind would be at ease.

Mirabel had one of her toys on the floor that she was batting it around. Wait a minute, I hadn't given her any toys!

I took it away from her. It was a post-it note.

It was a note from my Mum.

"Dear Aqua," it read. "I'm really sorry about our confrontation yesterday. When we see each other again we can discuss it. I have gone to the main New West bunker with our neighbours, as the news says that this is a level three infestation. It may get in the house. If you are reading this, it means you did not stay at work and are now holed up in our bunker. Please turn on the TV and they'll advise you when you can leave and join the main bunker. It's at Richmond Street and Eighth Avenue. Please come when you can. Love, Mum."

This was good news. My Mum was safe with our neighbours in the city bunker. I knew she could look after herself, and that I didn't have to worry about her.

The downside was that I may be stuck in this less than adequate bunker. Unless it rained, I would never be able to hoof it the six blocks over to the big city bunker, especially during a level three infestation. I must have just missed my Mum, as it had still been a level two when I had been taking the bus.

It was time to turn on the TV and check out what the newscasters had to say about our situation.

As I was fiddling with the remote I wondered where the blue weed had really come from. It couldn't be natural. It currently was only found in our part of the world. Was it some ghastly genetically-engineered plant experiment gone awry? If so, would the scientists ever own up to it? They would be hung, drawn, and quartered. This was a serious infestation of the third kind.

Or did the plant come from outer space? Was it carried here on a meteor that entered Earth's atmosphere, and then crashed to the ground? It may be worth doing an internet search once I was out of here. I had never really paid much attention to it. It was just here, and we dealt with it, much like getting a cold sore.

I found a local channel that was talking about the infestation. It started off with a brief moment of silence for those who lost their lives.

Of course. Here I am thinking about only myself, maybe my cat and Mum, when several humans have likely died outside today as they could not get under cover quickly enough, especially those unfortunate homeless souls. I took a two minute silence, then it was back to the business at hand.

"Good evening from the newsroom. This is

Sandeep. The Vancouver area has been hit with a bleed infestation not seen for over six months. It is recommended that everyone stay inside their personal bunkers. We'll keep you advised on the weather. Once it starts raining again it is advised that everyone evacuates to their nearest city bunker until the infestation has cleared. The Special Forces are currently suited up and tackling the bleed, metre by metre. A spokesman for the Forces said "no comment" when asked how long it would take to clear the latest bleed infestation from the Lower Mainland. When prompted, he said that they were focussing on Vancouver, the possible source of the latest mass infestation, and once that was done, they would consider moving onto New Westminster. Once again, stay tuned for the message to clear out from your personal bunkers and head to the main city bunker nearest you. Please bring all supplies with you in the event of a major lockdown."

I got tired of listening so I switched the sound off. The picture remained, along with the long banner of updates along the bottom. I certainly wouldn't be missing anything.

Mirabel and I had canned food for dinner. Her tinned cat food smelled better than my cold tomato and beans. There was even a little sink on the left side of the wall so I was able to do clean up. I found a small spot for garbage. I decided to scrub the tins too, so they didn't start to smell. Who knew when the garbage could be disposed of?

Mirabel was flopped on the ground. She looked ready to pack it in for the night. It was time for me to pull out the bed. It came out from within a narrow drawer. The mattress was quite thin. The only other time we had needed the bunker was during the big lockdown six months ago. My Mum and I had stayed up that entire night with the cat. We had sat on the bed chatting about stuff. I wished she were here now so we could chat again. Shopping, clothes, cats, the medical field even. Perhaps not marine biology though.

Our big chat about my future would have to wait. Obviously she wasn't "done" discussing it. Did she want to reason with me and change my mind? Or was she willing to have me attend my first year of marine biology? Maybe she wanted me to take a break. I really hoped we could sort it out. We didn't have the sort of toxic mother-daughter relationship that some did.

I lay on the bunk and Mirabel snuggled beside me. I think she was happy to get off the floor and onto something soft. Her soft happy vibrations lulled me to sleep.

I heard a buzzing sound. I lifted my head. Where was I? Had I nodded off? I found the cell phone in my pants pocket and switched it on.

"Yes! The cell phones are working now. They must have boosted the signal."

"Heather, is that you?" I asked drowsily.

"Who else? I think they found a way to make some of the phones work, for at least a few minutes anyway. Where are you?"

"Holed up in our bunker, ready to move out when they say."

"Me too. I wished we were together. I should have pushed you harder to join me. What a dunce I was."

"No, that's alright, I understand. I needed to come home for my...."

I didn't have a chance to finish, as we were cut off. No chance for me to ask if she could get out here, or maybe I could go there? Did I really want to face my mother in the morning?

CHAPTER FOUR—REGULATE

The Aquaria Chronicles

I MUST HAVE DOZED OFF as I woke to Mirabel gently tapping my nose with her paw. I reached out a hand to scratch her neck. She purred softly. It was always lovely to wake up to my beautiful kitty. It was time to check out the weather on TV. Could I finally leave the bunker to go join my Mum at the large shelter in my city?

I pulled myself upright and stretched. The little camp bed wasn't too bad, as my muscles didn't seem to be protesting too badly. I switched the volume on the TV to high.

Everything had gone well last night. It had rained, so Sandeep wore a big smile on his face while his coworker held an umbrella for him.

"Here I am in front of the Vancouver Art Gallery. Last night it rained heavily, which calmed down much of the bleed infestation. There's nary a spot of blue infestation to be seen anywhere. The Force worked all night long to ensure that any patches were pulled out and exposed to the fluidic outburst."

This was great news. Yesterday had been quite troubling. The small weather symbol at the bottom of the screen held a tiny sunshine symbol.

Mirabel started pawing at me for her breakfast.

"Just a minute Mirabel. I'll open your cat food shortly."

"However," Sandeep continued on. "We are still under a heavy bleed warning. The authorities believe that there are hidden patches and don't believe we have found them all yet. It's strongly advised that everyone stay where they are, and keep outdoor activities to a minimum."

I flicked the TV off. I guess this was why I hadn't woken to my Mum coming home. No one was allowed to leave, visit home, and then go back again. I checked my clock and it said 8 a.m. I had a few hours.

I cleaned up the bunker and then gathered the trash and put it outside in the garbage can.

We started the day by having a good breakfast. I didn't know what kind of supplies were in the city bunker, so felt that we should have one good meal to tide us over for the rest of the day.

I made a hearty pancake breakfast for me, complete with freshly squeezed orange juice, and a fruit salad. The raspberry syrup was to die for. It was the kind from the Okanagan. Mirabel had her standard fare, but also got some leftover chicken my Mum had left in the fridge. I let her finish it up as it would just go bad otherwise, and in any event I didn't eat chicken.

I was seriously considering becoming a vegetarian. There was no nutritional reason to not do so. I'd be healthier in the long run. What I did with my body now meant good health when I was eighty. I'm sure Mirabel would not understand that, but cats weren't cut out to be vegetarians.

As I wandered around the house to check for infiltration, Mirabel tagged along at my feet. Occasionally, she'd mew for attention. I took care of what needed to be done around the house. None of the bleed had gotten in, so there was nothing to do there. When I peered out the windows, everything seemed to be fine.

Who would have known that only a few hours ago the city had been under a deadly warning of bleed? The stuff came and went faster than you could say the word "snow" in Vancouver.

I tried the landline telephone but it was dead. The cell phone had drained its battery, so I searched for a charger. The one I found didn't fit on a Nokia, it was an Apple charger. I left the phone on the table as it was useless now.

In any event, I was going to be seeing my Mum in less than an hour, so didn't really need to call her, did I? If she'd been able to, she would have already called me.

I briefly missed Heather, but we'd catch up again in a day or so. That was the great thing about being best friends, even if you didn't chat every day, they were still your best friend at the end of the week. We sure had a lot to catch up on. She'd be worried that I never had the chance to connect with my Mum last night. I'm sure she would encourage me to join her in North Vancouver if there were any chance that I wouldn't be able to meet up with her at the bunker later.

I pulled the blinds and all the drapes on the windows. It was one more barrier should any bleed seep into the house. I tried to think like an adult and decide if there anything else that needed to be done around my home.

I placed Mirabel back in her carrier, packed up my things in my duffel bag, and moved on out. My purse was squished in there too. It would be difficult carrying a ten pound cat in her carrier. Good thing it was only a few blocks up the road. I also carried a shopping bag full of food. The news had said to bring extra, just in case.

"Come on Mirabel, you and I have a date with the big city bunker."

We left the house, locking the door behind us.

Outside seemed like business as usual. It appeared that most people hadn't followed the recommendations from the news. Cars were on the street, pedestrians were walking their dogs. Many people carried luggage, preparing for the big lockdown tonight. No one seemed concerned, it was same old, same old. A few passers-by greeted me and said hi to the kitty. Mirabel voiced her displeasure at being locked up.

All right, I knew where the bunker was, but had

never actually seen an entrance above ground. So, I wasn't quite sure where we were going, or which side of the street to be on. As I neared Richmond and Eighth Avenue, I wondered where I was supposed to go. I took a break in front of an old house that was being raised in order to add a new floor. The yard was a mass of rubble. Obviously the entrance to the bunker was hidden. I walked straight to the end of the street.

Mirabel was getting heavy. I crossed the street and put her down. Maybe I had to go onto someone's property to find it? I waited for someone to pass by, as perhaps they would know.

One little old lady walked past, clutching her dog's leash in her hand. "Hi dear. The entrance is across the street, between the house and the tree." She pointed towards it for me.

"Do you mean along that little pathway there?"

"That's it dear. See you in a little bit." She and her dog wended their way down the road.

I crossed the street and walked down the tiny pathway. Of course. This little path led to an underground tunnel that brought one to the other side of the street. Eighth Avenue was particularly busy and it was impossible to cross the street. They had built this little tunnel so kids could safely cross the street underground on their way to school.

Somewhere along here was the entrance. About halfway along stood an tall imposing man, maybe a couple of years older than me.

Relieved, I dropped my bags and placed the cat carrier gently on the ground.

"Is this the entrance to the city bunker?" I asked.

"It is. Have you brought supplies?" He looked curiously at my bags.

I had a good look at him. He was dressed head to toe in army issue gear. He had a rather large machine gun strapped across his back. That was odd, we weren't in a war, only a infestation of plant life. Guns were quite useless against plants. Unless he knew something I didn't?

And why wasn't he moving aside to allow me entrance?

"Do I need the secret password or something?" He ignored me as he examined my supplies.

"Is this bag only clothes? I'll take this package of canned goods." He picked it up.

I was getting annoyed that he was pawing through my stuff.

"Sorry, but the cat isn't allowed inside." He frowned at me.

"What do you mean? The bunkers have always allowed pets!" I glared at him.

"Sorry, change in rules. There's not going to be enough room for pets, let alone humans, once we lock down tonight." I moved to grab my bag of food but he held fast to it.

Behind me a crowd was forming. I guess everyone had the same idea as me, to take cover and wait things out.

"So, I'm not allowed inside, is that you're saying?"

"You are, your cat isn't." He nodded at me. "Look, are you coming inside? There's a crowd gathering and everyone has to be screened."

"My mother is inside waiting for me. What are you going to tell her? What if I can't make it back in time?"

"Well, you could leave your cat out here."

"In her carrier? I don't think so." What an idiot, no one leaves a cat in their carrier.

"You could let her out. I'm sure she'd find her way home," he suggested.

"Yes, miss, can we pass?" The little old lady I had spoken to earlier asked me. She had her dog in her arms.

I backed up, grabbing my duffel bag and cat carrier. I reached for the bag of canned goods again, but he placed the bag behind him on the ground. Of all the nerve. He was stealing it from me. Was there any hope that the bag would actually reach my Mum?

"Do you hear that?" I said to the crowd of people gathering, as I walked back down the tunnel. "He will not allow pets in." The crowd murmured. The little old lady looked down at her dog worriedly. There must have been about twenty people waiting at this point in time.

I heard people whispering to each other, but only two of us actually had any pets.

"What's the hold up?" a man yelled.

"We want inside!" a woman cried. Somewhere, a baby started wailing.

Someone threw an apple and it hit the guard against the side of the head. Why were people so juvenile? Is this what the human race had come to? It was only a simple lockdown. We'd had dozens before today, and there would be many more to come. People should have this thing down pat now.

Someone in the crowd screamed. I glanced behind me. Oh really?

The guard moved forward, waving his machine gun menacingly in the air. The crowd gasped. Is he seriously pointing that thing at us? Well, not at anyone specifically, he was waving it up near the ceiling. Come on, this is Canada! We don't need crap like that here. This isn't a movie theatre folks. We don't need to pack our weapons like Americans.

"Listen up folks. The sooner you are inside, the safer you will be. It is a quarter to twelve. If you have pets, you'll have to return home, leave them there, then return back here. Only humans are welcome."

The crowd hushed up then. He did have a good point. Were we in? Were we out? Most of the people moved forward. The guard ignored me and continued on with his pathetic job. The lady with the dog fell back with me.

I was furious, but everyone ignored me. They pushed their way around me. The only other person with a pet was the little old lady. We left the tunnel and I saw her wave sadly as she returned home. I wondered if she would return to the bunker, or she'd decide to stay at home. I'd take her dog, but my hands were full.

Why didn't they have a bunker just for pets? That could be a good idea, except I'm not sure pet owners would have time to drop their pets off there, then leave for their own bunkers. It sounded good in theory. I guess it could be because pets were immune to the bleed. However, pets couldn't really feed or water themselves. A human had to help them out with those things.

As for us, I wasn't sure what to do. My mother would be worried sick if I never showed up at the bunker. Or would she figure that I had decided to stay in Vancouver? Should we just go home? There was nowhere else to go. We'd just have to take our chances that we'd be safe in our home bunker. There was no way I'd have time to return before they locked up at noon. Perhaps the telephones were working now, and Mum could leave me a message? Did they have a landline in the city bunker? And probably a kilometre long line of people to use it. It would overflow with quarters before the line dissipated. I giggled.

I paused at the exit to the bunker. I couldn't

believe that moron stole our food. Wait until this warning was over. I'd be calling the mayor with my complaint, and demanding a full refund of my food.

I'll bet the bunker in North Vancouver allowed pets. I should have convinced her to drive to New West to grab my cat, and then head to North Van while I had the chance. Her house bunker was probably quite adequate and they could hole up there for weeks on end if they had to.

Briefly I wished I could contact someone that I knew for advice. Here I was stuck with a cat, and nowhere to go. Thoughts of being holed up in a six foot by four foot room for days on end didn't thrill me. It wouldn't be more than a day would it?

I was standing there like an idiot while my neighbours filtered into the underground tunnel. I recognized a few, but didn't know anyone by name. Or, if I had known their names, I certainly didn't remember.

I picked up my stuff and walked down the outer pathway. I was just passing the house on my right when I heard a cry for help.

"Hello?" I called. "Does someone need assistance? I'm trained in Level Three First Aid."

"Help!" a guy's voice called. "I'm down here." The sound seemed to be coming from the house beside me. It was below the embankment before me, sliding down on a gentle slope. All I could see were masses of those bushes that reek of dog piss.

I moved forward to get a closer look. Way down past the bushes I could see a patch of grass in front of the house. Lying below was a guy about my age wearing slacks and a burgundy dress shirt, sprawled on the ground. A wheelchair was haphazardly lying askew beside him. He waved up at me.

CHAPTER FIVE—HYPERVENTILATE

The Aquaria Chronicles

I FOUND THE STEPS leading down to the house. Once down on the lower level I left my bag and cat carrier on the ground. I'm not sure what mischief this guy had gotten up to, but it was my duty to make sure he wasn't injured.

"Hello," I said to him, edging closer. I had a quick look around. The first rule of first aid was to make sure that the location was safe. I didn't see any hovering aliens or rabid dogs so I walked up to him.

"My name is Aqua and I am trained in Level Three First Aid. Are you okay?" I leaned down towards him.

"Well, other than being booted out of my wheelchair, I think I'm okay. I can pull myself back into my chair, but I had a panic attack and thought I might be injured."

"What's your name?" I asked him. He was an attractive dark haired guy around my age, perhaps about sixteen years old.

"My name is Mark," he said, in a cute voice.

"Okay Mark, I'm going to check for broken bones before I move you. Did you hit your head at all? How is your breathing?"

"No, I didn't hit my head. I can breathe just fine,

thanks."

I examined his head, and he was right, I could not see any contusions. I checked his neck, went down to his shoulders, checked his arms and legs. Front seemed good, I felt with my hands behind his body.

He started giggling.

"What is it?" I asked.

He seemed a bit embarrassed.

"I don't think anyone besides my Mum has ever touched me before."

"Okay," I said. "This is totally necessary, and rest assured, I wouldn't touch you if I didn't have to."

"I know, no one does," he said sighing.

"Oh no! I don't mean it that way, I meant I don't go poking and prodding guys if I don't have to." I giggled. "I'm sure you are quite lovely to touch in normal circumstances."

"Oh good," he said, smiling a little.

"So, nothing hurts?" I asked.

He shook his head.

I checked his feet. I couldn't see anything wrong.

"What exactly happened?" I asked him, before attempting to move him into an upright position.

"I was pushed down the embankment."

"What?" I was outraged. "By whom?"

He motioned his head above him. "By the guard at the gate."

"Are you serious? The guard at the city bunker?

They're sworn to protect us, not injure us."

"I don't know what happened Aqua. Pretty name by the way. I wheeled myself out here from my house, which is just a few houses down. I came here to meet my parents, but I guess they had already gone inside. I showed up at the entrance. The guard flat out refused my entrance when he had a good look at my wheelchair."

"What were his words?" I asked him. "He refused to give my cat entrance, but he would have let me inside."

Mark looked embarrassed. I didn't know if that was a common occurrence for him in dealing with a permanent disability. I helped raise him to a sitting position. I wanted to leave him like this for few minutes, just to be sure he hadn't sustained any internal injuries.

"Well, he said wheelchairs weren't allowed."

"That's an abomination. What is with that stupid guard? He's running on his own orders. When this lockdown is over, I'm calling City Hall and having a few words with the mayor."

He watched me with his bright brown eyes as I harangued onwards.

"Excuse me for interrupting you, but could you help me back into my wheelchair?"

"Sure. Is there a way out of here that doesn't involve me carrying you up the stairs?" I looked around the yard.

"Yes, around the back. It leads straight to the alley. We can get onto the street from there."

I righted his wheelchair and led it towards him. Once his hands touched the wheelchair he was able to pull himself into it. I found a messenger bag lying on the ground and handed that to him.

"Before we move out, I think we need to discuss where we are going. I imagine that by now all bunkers are on lockdown. They won't allow us entry."

Mark nodded. "We could head for home but I'm concerned that if another bleed storm comes, that we won't be safe there. That's why they were recommending that we head for the big city bunker."

I nodded. "That's right. Well, I don't think we have much choice but to head for home. Why don't we exchange information and I'll check on you in a day or so?"

Mark moved his head in the negative. "Nope, I have a better idea."

"What is it?" I asked him. Mirabel was starting to get restless in her carrier and I wanted to get her out as soon as possible.

Just at that moment we heard gunfire coming from the direction of the bunker entrance. I wheeled Mark around the left side of the house. I didn't know what was happening, but we didn't need to sustain any bullet wounds.

Why had I come this way? It was nonstop fun at the New Westminster bunker. Come inside if you pass their impossible test, then get shot.

"What is happening?" Mark whispered at me.

"I'm not sure," I whispered back. "I wonder if someone got mad at their Nazi rules and is trying to barge their way in."

I peered around the corner. I could see absolutely nothing from here. Plus, I was horrified to discover that I had left Mirabel on the ground by the steps.

I crawled out on my hands and knees. I still heard commotion coming from above me. I carefully grabbed the carrier and my duffel bag, and snuck back to Mark.

He took the carrier and my bag and balanced them on his lap.

"I think I need to go in for a closer look. See what's going on."

Mark grabbed my arm.

"Please don't go. If they have weapons you could be injured. I have no way of helping you. My cell phone has been dead since yesterday."

"My Mum's in that bunker. I have to make sure she's safe." Without another word I snuck back into the front yard. All seemed quiet above me. I slowly and quietly climbed the steps leading back to the top of the sidewalk.

I checked left and right.

There was a body lying on the ground. I had a

quick look around, then moved forward. I could detect no pulse or breathing. The man was dead from a bullet wound to the chest.

What had happened here? What was going on? This was supposed to be a simple outbreak of a plant plague, but we had a bunker locked up tight with dead bodies. I slipped down the pathway to the bunker. No one was around. I peered into the inner passageway of the tunnel. The lights were glaring, but I didn't see anything ahead. Should I risk heading in? I couldn't see anything anywhere.

I made my decision. My Mum was locked in that bunker and I had to make sure she was safe. As I neared the entrance to the bunker I saw another male body lying on the ground. A quick check told me that he was as dead as his colleague outside.

So it appeared to me that perhaps they had both been seeking entrance to the bunker. But why? And why wouldn't the guard let them in?

Out of options, I decided my last course of action was to actually knock on the bunker door.

There was no response. I wondered if a camera was outside here, and sure enough there was. I waved at the camera I saw.

"Hello, my name is Aqua. My mother is locked inside. I'm concerned for her safety and welfare. There are bodies scattered on the ground out here. I know you can't open up, but can you give me some indication that all is well within? You can even keep my bag of food, I don't care."

The silence from behind the door was absolute. It was no use. There was no communication. I decided to hightail it out of there, in case more gunmen showed up.

I had a quick look around, making certain that no one was hiding from my view. I didn't want any surprises, nor did I want to lead anyone back to Mark and Mirabel.

I had an uneventful jog back to them.

"What's happening out there?" Mark asked. He had his fingers inside the cat carrier to stroke Mirabel. She was lying there purring contentedly. Her needs were being taken care of for the moment but she'd already been in that cat carrier for too long.

"As near as I can figure, a couple of men tried to break their way into the bunker. There are two dead bodies lying on the ground."

Mark looked shocked. "Was there anyone alive out there? Hiding?"

"I don't think so. Whatever scuffle they had seems to be over. I'm shocked that anyone would try to force their way in. How did they know to bring guns? Or is something else going on inside that bunker?"

"My parents are inside there," Mark said. He looked worried.

"So is my Mum. I really hope they are safe inside.

I'm a bit worried at the attitude of that one guard though. Was he trying to do his job, or was he protecting something within?"

"Our parents could be at their mercy," Mark sobbed. I liked him immediately. You had to admire a guy who let a little bit of emotion show. And a guy who loved and respected his parents was worth knowing.

"Mark, we're going to have to get away from here. Whatever is going on, it could get worse. Someone might show up with tanks next. What if they have the entire supply of gold in there?"

"That's silly Aqua. You have quite the imagination. If anything, their supplies are gold."

"What?"

"Their water. Their food, medical supplies. It could be gold to someone if the apocalypse were coming."

I shook my head. Unbelievable. He accuses me of an imagination and look how he sounds.

"Mark, now you are fantasizing."

"Think about it Aqua. Why would people die to get inside a bunker? Perhaps they know something we don't. We haven't even been near a phone, radio or TV for hours. We don't know what is happening. There could be another bleed infestation coming."

I looked around me. The air was dry and the trees and grass had dried off after the great downpour last night.

"Do you live near here?" I asked him.

"Yep, you can see my house from here."

"All right then, it's much closer than mine is. I think we need to head to your house and listen to the news."

"Great idea Aqua. Let's head for home, and we can get some idea of what to do next. I also have an idea of what to do after that too."

He wouldn't let me wheel him down the alley. His wheelchair was fully motorized so we headed to his house. I made a brief note to make sure we charged up his wheelchair in case we had to leave to go somewhere else. I wasn't sure where else that would be though.

His house was a bit more modest than mine but still appeared to be comfortable. I left him fiddling with the remote control. He managed to find the news. Sandeep Singh looked dismayed.

Mark turned the sound up.

"It's recommended that people go to their nearest city bunker and stay there. The botanists have been doing tests on the blue weed, or more commonly known as the bleed. Apparently it's mutating into a far more dangerous form. People are requested to stay indoors. All malls are deemed closed as of now, and cars will be pulled over on the streets in about an hour's time. Residents have less than an hour to final lockdown."

Mark had seen enough. He shut off the TV.

"Well, that answers that question. That massive fall

we had yesterday was from the bleed mutating."

"Great. I hope your bunker is big enough, because mine can barely hold a cat and a human."

I'd let Mirabel out of her carrier so she was happily washing herself on the sofa. I'd get some food and a litter box set up for her shortly.

Mark was seated in his wheelchair. He didn't look well. I moved closer.

He seemed to be wheezing, like he was having some difficulty breathing.

"Mark, are you all right?" He was wheezing more rapidly now.

I looked around the room for some sort of medication.

"Grab my bag over there," he said in between gasps.

I found his blue messenger bag and brought it over. I opened it up for him. It was filled with books and a small laptop. At the bottom I saw a small inhaler, so I dug it out and handed it to him.

I think it was just in time, as he appeared to be turning blue.

"Hurry, Mark!"

He popped off the lid, inserted it into his mouth and pressed the button. A fine mist was released. He breathed in as deeply as he could. His colouring started returning to normal. He then pulled out a small paper bag from a small pouch on his wheelchair and started breathing into it.

"I'm hyperventilating now, I'm all stressed out. It's in the room with us," he said.

"What is Mark?" I glanced around me.

"The bleed. Some must have gotten in."

I looked near the window. He was right. The window seals had failed.

"We need to get into the shelter, Mark". I motioned to the door.

"I have a better idea," he said.

I put Mirabel back into the carrier. She meowed and seemed a bit outraged that she was going back in without completing her bath.

"We can go to this other massive bunker that I heard about."

"What? Where is it?"

"I think it's on Eighth Avenue and Ovens."

I shook my head. "Mark, in case you haven't noticed, it's not safe for you to be out there. I may be temporarily immune to the bleed, but if you go out there, you are going to have another asthma attack."

"There's no option. This latest infestation of bleed is too powerful. We are going to have to go to a safe house."

He was right. The bleed seemed to be covering the windows, like it was alive and wanted to get inside our lungs.

CHAPTER SIX—DISCOMBOBULATE

The Aquaria Chronicles

MARK AND I WERE RAPIDLY TRYING TO PREPARE to leave. I decided I had to let Mirabel out of her carrier for a pee and a dish of cat food. Mark wasn't ready anyway. The wheelchair slowed him down. He wanted to collect some essentials, as he wasn't certain how well-prepared a research facility would be.

He wrote a note for his parents to let them know we hadn't made it inside the New West bunker, and that we were heading to a research facility. Apparently it was only two blocks away, which was a lot closer than my house. Hopefully it actually existed and we would have better luck there. He also left contact information for my Mum, in case they were able to contact her somehow. It was a long shot, but we covered all the bases.

I sorted through my purse and duffel bag. Mark handed me some bags of cookies and bottles of water, so I squished them in. Yes, we were ready to survive the apocalypse with our cookies and water.

Mark solemnly passed me some paring knives.

"For weapons," he said, "just in case."

I tucked them into the side pockets of my bag. That should keep me from cutting myself.

"Where did you hear of this bunker?" I asked him.

"At school. Our teacher said he was involved in researching sea creatures on a ship, like the ones that ate up all the iron on the Titanic wreck. They have an underground research facility set up in New West. Apparently there is no longer any cheap above-ground real estate to be had, so many companies are choosing to build underground now."

"Really? I hope I get to meet him. I'm fascinated with all forms of sea life." I smiled at the thought.

"You should get along with him then, he's quite the ladies man," Mark said, winking at me.

"Oh, no, not in that way. I have no time for guys. I'm supposed to be at university next week." I was horrified beyond belief.

"Really?" Mark said, zipping up his bag and placing it on his lap. "Do you think everything will be back to normal next week?"

"I hope so, otherwise none of us will need to worry about our career paths ever again."

He nodded his head agreeing to that.

"I think we should get going," he said, looking outside. A light rain had started falling. That would be our salvation in walking, or wheeling in his case, the several blocks to the next bunker. Transit would likely have stopped by now.

I picked up my stuff, including the cat carrier, and went onto the porch. Mark grabbed a face mask off the kitchen table before he left the house. I watched him lock up. He wheeled himself ahead of me, heading down his wheelchair ramp.

"Who built this? Is it cedar? Look at the carvings. They even carved some lions for the entrance."

"My Dad did. He's a good carpenter. It's also what he does for a living. He's equipped our home for me in many clever ways."

I had noticed the carved hand rails in the bathroom earlier. What a marvel they were.

The light rain was still falling. We travelled for several minutes in silence. The end of the world was exhausting.

"Do you really know where we are going?" I asked him.

"I have a pretty good clue. I hear it's quite something to see." He pointed ahead.

"Great! Can't wait. I do hope the guards are friendlier."

He chuckled. "I'm sure they are, if they're anything like my teacher."

"Are you still in high school?" I asked him.

"Final year, what about you?" He smiled up at me. I knew he was younger.

"I finished two years ago, in the gifted program."

"So, what are you taking in university?" he asked me, suitably impressed. His wheelchair made a light buzzing sound. We'd had about twenty minutes to charge it up earlier. I hoped it would last throughout the day.

We approached Eighth Avenue. Only a few more blocks, I hoped.

"I started in a Bachelor of Science. Next week I'm starting Marine Biology."

"That's neat," he said. "I might go in for that too. You really need to meet Mr. Owens."

"Finally, something to look forward to, after these last two pathetic days I've had."

I had to stop to take a break. Mirabel protested when I placed her on the ground. She liked the motion of me carrying her cat carrier. I placed the duffel bag down too.

There were still cars on the road. People had this panicked look on their faces. We saw a few fender benders along the way. No one was driving safely. I think walking was a safer mode of transportation, as long as we carefully crossed the streets. We walked past a couple of men arguing about the dents in their cars. That was what insurance was for. What was wrong with people? Soon the air would be flooded again. They should get under cover. There wasn't much time left. That may be my decision, but then I wasn't an ignorant person.

In fact, I was getting worried myself. I hope my Mum and Heather were safely indoors. It was only a crazy twist of fate that I wasn't with either of them.

Having a cat was a big responsibility—a lifelong commitment. I'd give my life for my cat. If she died, I'd die too. I knelt down to check on her. She was sleeping, so that was a good thing. A cat wouldn't miss out on her nap even if she were travelling. Best to do it now—it might be a crazy evening later, with plenty of noise. Definitely not conducive to cat naps.

We decided to get going again. I was counting down the minutes. If this were a research facility though, they likely would let us in at any time. There really was no deadline. I picked up the carrier in one hand, and the duffel bag in another.

"Do you want me to take one of those?" Mark asked. He pointed at the bag.

"No, I might as well get used to carrying them. Who knows how much travelling we're going to need to do today?" I had a quick look at the sky but all seemed well.

As we were crossing Eighth Avenue at Cumberland, we heard footsteps running from behind us. I didn't think much of it at first. There were a few people on the street, likely heading for home to prepare for the big lock up. They sounded like they were in a hurry. Perhaps we could add to our party of two. It would be nice to have some extra company along the way. We stopped and turned to look. Mark looked cautiously at me and wiggled his finger at my bag.

A grubby man came rushing up from behind. He

looked disheveled and dirty but his clothes might have been clean a few days ago, as they were office wear. He wore slacks, what was once a white shirt, and a disheveled tie. I could smell him from even a few feet away.

He gave me a hard shove and I went sprawling on the ground. What the?! What had just happened? Had he PUSHED me? What was wrong with him? So much for a friendly party of three.

"Hey," Mark yelled. "What do you think you're doing?"

Mirabel's cage landed with a thump on the ground. I had whacked my elbow and I winced but there was nothing broken. I quickly glanced at my cat but she looked fine besides being annoyed from waking up from her nap.

I checked to make sure Mark was all right. He appeared to be quite flustered.

I looked just in time to see the evil man kicking Mark.

"Give me your food and water!" he screamed at us.

The man was clearly mad. Did we no longer live in civilized society?

"Whoa there Nelly," I said. "This violence is unnecessary. We can share what we have." I pointed to our grocery bag. Plenty of stuff to share in there.

"You asshole," Mark cried, as the man hit him in the face. "Why don't you break into a house like rest of your kind?" He waved his fist at the man.

This was unbelievable. We were under attack! I scrambled to my bag that held the knives. Great, we had all sorts of things happen to us, and now a crazy man was attacking us for food. Did he know there was an entire grocery store down the street, and likely unguarded? There'd be no one there at this time. He could just help himself if he had an aversion to paying. What a crazy day this had been.

"Give me the bag!" he yelled at Mark. He was heading towards Mark again.

Mark was trying to apply power to his wheelchair and steer himself backwards. I don't think he was going to give up the bag that easily.

My elbow was a bit sore from landing on the ground and boy was I getting aggravated. No wait, I was already aggravated. I pulled the knife out of my bag. He didn't even see me coming. I dropped to a kneeling position.

I shoved the knife into the back of his knee with my right hand. It went in easily.

He howled and screamed and fell to the ground. He writhed and cried. I didn't have much pity for him as he had attacked both of us first.

I made sure Mark was fine. He had a black eye and a bruise on his leg but nothing that required immediate medical attention. We grabbed our things and took off. I glanced behind us, but that kind of injury would keep him laid up for a very long time. I'd lost one of our knives, so hopefully we wouldn't come across much more trouble.

"I think the bleed is affecting people's brains," Mark said.

"What? You mean, like zombies?" I took a quick glance at the man on the ground, but he appeared to be harmless for the moment.

"I don't know, but his eyes were glowing blue. I think we need to get indoors before the bleed starts floating again."

We gathered up our belongings and took one last look behind us. I was fairly certain that we wouldn't be followed. One look at the man on the ground and it was confirmed that even if he managed to remove the knife from his kneecap, he'd still have to stop the bleeding and deal with the pain. Excellent.

We crossed McBride Avenue. There were actually quite a few cars on the road. Did they know that the apocalypse was coming? Apparently not.

"It's just across the street. We're almost there," Mark said, reassuring me.

"Great! I think it's taken us longer to get from your place to the facility, than it took me to get from the Aquarium to my home yesterday."

We got going again. It was fast going after that. We saw the grocery store up ahead. Sure enough, there were no guards there. People had already resorted to looting and grabbing. None of them were paying much attention to us. I watched a couple load a large cooling fan and a TV into a car. Really? Are those things even going to work if the electricity goes out? All the power would be diverted to the bunkers shortly. I don't even think you could take a TV into a bunker. What a big waste of energy it would be.

Mark brought his wheelchair to a stop. I started looking where he was looking. We were gazing over a large condo development. On our end, only the pit had been dug, and the concrete poured. On the other side a four story condo was going up. It was framed, but it hadn't even been roofed or sided yet. Come to think of it, this development had been happening for the past two years. It sure was taking a long time to build.

"Here it is," Mark said.

"Where?" I asked. "Here?"

"Right here."

"All I see is a condo development that isn't too far along."

"I know, let's get going."

We crossed the street.

"So, is there a hidden entrance to this one too?"

"Apparently there is. Remember I told you that the bunker is underground? This is a research facility. They had to build underground, as it was a lot cheaper than leasing something on the surface. Besides, the sea creatures don't care if there is direct sunlight or not."

"Sea creatures? Well, this won't be a complete loss then. I get to talk to your teacher, plus meet sea creatures? Did I mention that I was in?"

Mark looked up at me and smiled. This was going to be a great adventure. At least, once we found out where the entrance was. The development encompassed several acres. It was going to be fun finding the entrance. Far more difficult than finding the entrance of the New Westminster city bunker.

"Where do we start?" I asked him.

Mark looked a bit worried. The ground surrounding the development did not look wheelchair friendly. I also didn't relish climbing over all the two by fours, with duffle bag and cat in tow.

"I think we should split up," Mark suggested. "We can meet back here in fifteen minutes."

"Well, that sounds like a plan," I replied. "Why don't we leave our things here? There is a good hiding spot here and I think my cat will be safe for a bit. I won't go out of viewing distance of her in any case."

Mark dropped the bag of groceries and his messenger bag on the ground. I tucked them underneath the pile of wood beams. He took off along the sidewalk. If he was covering the sidewalk that meant that I had to cover the spaces that weren't paved, as his wheelchair would never be able to traverse them.

I started heading towards the main entrance of the building when I felt the bleed start to fall softly from the sky. I put my face mask over my nose and mouth. I knew Mark had his face mask so didn't bother going after him to remind him to put it on. He was a big boy and could look after himself.

Okay, where to start? The bunker was underground, so I needed go to the first level to look.

CHAPTER SEVEN—STARGATE

The Aquaria Chronicles

I ENTERED THROUGH THE MAIN DOOR
of the development even though I could have entered through any of the patios. The building had only reached the framing stage, built over a concrete base. I wandered around a bit, but really didn't think there would be any door into the ground. It didn't take long to walk a circle around the entire building. I had nearly given up when I heard a sound off to the side.

I wondered if it were Mark but I didn't think he could get his wheelchair into this area. I ducked behind a pile of two by fours. It was obvious that I heard footsteps. They came closer. Whoever it was knew that I was on the property.

"Come out come out from wherever you are. I know there is someone here," said a menacing voice.

I could have whacked myself over the head. I had left our one remaining knife in my backpack. I had no weapons on me. Was it possible there was something I could use in this construction mess?

Where was Mark anyway? Had he encountered this person yet? Perhaps not, as he was only driving around the outer perimeter of the building, on the sidewalk. Obviously this person knew I wasn't supposed to be here. Hopefully he hadn't encountered Mark, or harmed him.

I had a look around. A hammer was within easy reach, so I slowly picked it up, not making a sound.

"I know there's someone in here! Ah hah!"

The man had come upon my hiding spot. He seemed like a normal man dressed in a security guard's uniform. Should I trust him, when I had had problems with the other one? I slowly raised myself to a standing position, obscuring the hammer behind my back.

"Well well well," said the man. "What do we have here?"

"It's not what, it's who. And I'm here to find the research bunker. I'm not certain of the entrance, however. If you can steer me in the correct direction, that would be great."

"Research bunker? No such thing around here. You're trespassing."

"I know. In case you hadn't noticed, we are on lockdown, and I'm trying to find a bunker to hole up in."

"I don't think so. More than likely you have come here to steal tools." He leered at me.

"Yah right. If I was going to do that, I'd go to the nearest Canadian Tire, not a crappy old construction site that's been here for years without anything ever being built on it."

"There's a hammer behind your back," the guard

said. He walked up closer. I shuddered to see his eyes glow a luminescent blue colour. Could the bleed be affecting him?

He grabbed my arm and squeezed. I think he must have bruised some muscles and tendons as I let out a gasp. I wasn't injured enough to not think of swinging my hammer arm around though. It connected to his skull with a loud splat.

Down he went. His body then started going into paroxysms. That little tap should have rendered him unconscious but it didn't. As he rolled around on the floor, his tongue lolled out. He started foaming at the mouth. I really didn't want to be around to see what would happen next. I raced through the patio opening onto the sidewalk.

"Aqua! I heard strange noises. Are you okay?"

"No, while you were away I was being attacked by a zombie!"

"Really? Are those things for real?" Mark wheeled himself closer for a better look.

"Yes, really. His eyes glowed blue, and when I whacked him on the skull with a hammer, he fell and started acting weird, tongue lolling, spasming, rolling around on the ground."

"Wow, well I've heard that's how you kill a zombie. You either hack off their head or destroy their brain. I imagine you just injured it."

I breathed a sigh of relief that I hadn't killed him.

Wasn't this just fantastic? This was the best Saturday ever. I couldn't even begin to write a book on all that I had gone through today.

Mark tapped my arm to bring me out of my reverie.

"I think we need to continue our search. Have you had any luck in finding a doorway?"

"No, there was nothing inside. The entire surface of concrete was unblemished. There is no way that there is a door in the floor. How about you, have you found anything?"

"Possibly, but there are no doors going into the building, and nothing from the sidewalk. Whoever designed the bunker has cleverly concealed the entrance."

"You know what, I'm exhausted. I wonder how much time we have left?"

"I know. Have you noticed that the drizzle has stopped? Back on the north side I noticed a tiny patch of bleed growing underneath the eaves of the building beside this one." Mark pointed in the general direction.

"Well, that's just great. If it's that super mutated version, it's going to be humongous in about an hour."

"It definitely is. I couldn't find any water faucets anywhere to try and tame it."

"I didn't even think of that. Perhaps we should have brought some bottles with us just in case. I even forgot my knife and I could have definitely used it earlier."

We peered intently at the sky. As if one cue, a light dusting of bleed fell softly down. Mark had pulled out his mask and placed it over his nose faster than I could have warned him to.

I yanked my mask up over my nose too. This was beginning to be a common occurrence. Hell, it was already a common occurrence.

"Aqua, I think we should return for the cat and our luggage. I have a hunch that the entrance could be from the mechanical room, which is along the back northern side of the building."

I followed him along the sidewalk.

"How many hours of power do you have in your chair?" I asked him.

He looked down at the controls on his chair.

"Oh, about four I believe. I should have enough until we can get inside, and I can recharge. Don't worry about me."

We hoofed it back along the sidewalk, past the building, then past the big empty pit in the ground. I really hoped that the bunker door wasn't down there, as I didn't want to muss my shoes, and I had no idea how I would get Mark down there in his wheelchair.

We finally had reached the opposite end of the building. I was keeping an eye out for the creepy zombie guy, but didn't see him again. I pulled Mirabel's carrier out from under the boards. She looked none the worse for wear. I think she had been napping. I gave Mark his messenger bag and the bag of groceries, and flung the strap of my duffel bag over my shoulder. We were back on our way again.

"I suggest we go around the plot this way. It will be a faster way to get to the back." Mark led the way. I followed as his wheelchair traversed the pebbled sidewalk. He bounced around a bit, but did well enough that he didn't tip over. We reached what was a back alley, though it was roped off front and back. The construction workers were using it for storage. I pulled down the rope so Mark could get past.

We stopped for a bit.

"I think we should be careful before we enter," he said to me in a whisper.

"You're right. Even if there aren't any more zombies around, there could be a security guard like at the last place."

I tiptoed along the alley while he ran his wheelchair at half power. It took longer but it paid to be careful. We ducked behind a tree or two along the way.

"Do you see up ahead? There is a large metal cabinet."

"Yes, I do." It was painted a dark green colour.

"That's where they normally store the mechanical room for everything that runs a building. The a.c., the water pump, the heater."

"Oh clever. You think the door we need is behind

door number one?"

Mark laughed, then stopped, horrified. Had anyone heard us?

We gazed around worriedly. Nope, I don't think there was a soul around. We crept closer.

As we were creeping, the fine mist of bleed came down heavier. We shook ourselves off like cats. Whether we liked it or not we were going to have to get into that mechanical room and stay there.

"Why don't we hoof it to the door?"

Mark nodded back.

I raced up ahead, with Mark on full speed. I reached the door of the metal cabinet in seconds. Mark came in a close second right behind me. I dropped the heavy supplies on the ground. Mark dropped his packs on the ground too. They were getting too heavy to carry. I fiddled with the lock on the cabinet.

"I can't believe it's locked," Mark said. "We need to get under cover soon."

"I know. I can hack it with that pairing knife." I dug through the outer pockets of my bag until I found the knife. It took me seconds to pop open the padlock.

"Where'd you learn how to do that?" Mark asked.

"In high school. Some of the kids broke into my locker so I had to retaliate."

"Hmm," Mark mused. "I must learn how to do that too."

"Well, I'll teach you, but right now our safety is

more important." I swung open the door. In we went.

"Do you have a flashlight? It's mighty dark in here."

I heard Mark going through one of his bags.

"Sure do." He manually wheeled himself over. I'm not sure if he could control his wheelchair to the centimetre. I imagine that in some cases it was easier to release the wheel lock and roll away.

"It's bigger on the inside than the outside," I said jokingly.

"Awesome," he said.

I flashed the light around.

He tapped my arm.

"I think we should bring our stuff in, lock the doors and start exploring."

"Good point," I replied. I helped him go out and grab the stuff. I think Mirabel was itching to get out of her carrier too.

I discovered that we could also padlock the door from the inside, so I did. I then let Mirabel out of her carrier.

No sooner was she out then she squatted in the corner.

"Oh god, I thought dogs stank, but pee-yew!" said Mark.

"Oops, sorry. I'm surprised she held it for so long. I'll go clean it up."

Afterwards we explored the small metal box. There

wasn't much to it. The usual air conditioner, heating system, and plumbing equipment.

"There has to be the entrance to the research facility in here somewhere," stated Mark.

"Well, I've looked along the ground, the ceiling, and the four walls. I simply don't see anything." Mirabel started tapping me on the leg. I think it was time for her dinner.

I think it was time for our dinner. It had been a long day. We fed and watered ourselves. We were starting to yawn, but I think we both unanimously agreed that we would both stay awake long enough to figure out where that research bunker was. Even if it meant moving out again.

"If we don't find it tonight, I think we need to go back to my place and stay there until the morning. In the morning we can figure out what to do," I suggested.

"Wow," Mark said smiling. "A girl has never invited me back to her place before."

"What the?" I started saying. Then I swatted him as he had a big smile on his face. He was obviously joking. He was a great guy, but I was going back to school next week. I didn't need a boyfriend.

We were having another look around when we heard a banging noise coming from outside the entrance to the room.

"That can't be good," I said.

"I'll find some weapons," Mark said.

I started poking around the plumbing. It was a mass of pipes. We hadn't had a good look earlier as it was a busy area. There had to be something around here, right?

A huge pounding hit the door. I looked back. A huge concave dent appeared in the door. Someone on the other side had rammed something into it.

"Hurry," Mark said. "Have you found anything?" He was rounding up the cat and our equipment.

"I'm trying!" I said as my voice broke. I leaned against a narrow pipe to take a break. I was truly exhausted. Would the nightmare never end?

As I leaned against the pipe, it slid towards the wall. A loud creaking noise was heard. A small door slid open in the wall.

"Mark! I've found it," I said happily.

He came racing forward. We just had time to grab our stuff and get through the doorway, when the metal door behind us burst open.

Ahead of us, another door opened in the wall. A group of uniformed people massed out and ran around us. We stepped aside.

Loud gunfire was heard behind us. We crouched down near the floor. It sounded like they were attacking the zombie man who had come after me earlier.

The racket quietened down. I watched as a couple of the people started clearing up the damage in preparation to fix the breach.

A woman beckoned us forward.

"Don't worry about that mess. It will all be cleaned and repaired. You must come inside. You both look like you're exhausted."

"We are," I said gratefully.

"Is this the research bunker?" Mark asked.

"Why, yes it is. My name is Joyce. I'm one of the marines here. We are a part of the new Canadian MCR —Marine Commando Regiment. I'll take you to see Stephen. He'll be thrilled that a few more humans made it."

"What do you mean made it?" I asked. "What has happened?"

"A lot of humans have died these past couple of days from the bleed infestation," Joyce explained.

We followed her down a narrow corridor that was lit with tiny battery-operated torches.

"There have been many who have gone crazy. We think that it's caused by a bleed mutation. Unfortunately, there is nothing we can do for them at the moment. If they leave us alone, we leave them alone. If they attack, we attack."

Mark and I gazed in wonder at each other.

"Does this mean that we have joined the marines?" Mark asked.

Joyce laughed. "Well, it takes a bit more than that, but if you want to, we sure could use the help."

"A lot has happened in forty-eight hours," I said to

Mark. He nodded.

A thought occurred to me. "I have my cat in this carrier. Are we welcome in the bunker?"

"Why, yes of course. Everyone is welcome here. We have been trying to keep an eye out for survivors caught in the storm."

"That's great, thank you," I said to her. Finally, some friendly folk. I felt momentarily guilty for not asking about whether Mark was welcome here, but obviously he was, as Joyce grabbed one of Mark's bags to help him out.

Joyce led us to an elevator. She punched in a code and the doors opened. She took us first to be decontaminated in the showers. After we had towelled off and had fresh clothes we were led back to the elevators.

We entered. We were happy that we were finally away from the storm outside. The elevator quickly descended. I had no idea how far down we went.

The doors of the elevator opened onto paradise. Joyce told us to step off and enter the chamber. We did, dropping our things on the floor. We gazed up at the beauty surrounding us.

The entire building was filled top, bottom and centre with aquariums and sea life. I gazed at the floor below me. It was one giant aquarium. I saw huge beluga whales swimming below me. It was an odd feeling of standing over water. If I gazed far enough below, perhaps one-hundred metres, I could see rock formations. A variety of beluga whales swam around the tank. At least I think it was a tank, perhaps we were seated above the ocean? One white baby beluga was curious about the new arrivals and swam close to the top of the tank. I waved at her.

"Look Mark," I said, pointing to the whale. He turned on his wheels and had a look.

We watched the whales frolicking in the water. I had never seen so many at once before, but it appeared they were hanging out in this one spot. When I peered beyond I could see that they had a vast amount of space to swim around in. So much greater than any aquarium ever had. For the first time that day I actually smiled, enjoying their playful antics. I could watch them for hours, but then Mark pointed skyward.

Up above us was a ceiling containing an aquarium. It must have been about five stories up the wall. Smaller fish and sea creatures lived in these tanks. I couldn't wait to explore. I saw many species that I recognized and many I didn't. Some were salt water fish in their tanks, and some were fresh water fish in their own tanks. They swam together in schools of fish. These fish didn't have the entire ceiling tank to themselves. I noticed that they were segregated into small tanks, probably giving them a better chance for survival.

"Look at all the fish. We'll have a great time exploring this building Mark. It's like one huge aquarium."

I smiled at him. He smiled back.

"I think Mirabel might have the time of her life too. I hope she can't get into any of the tanks. That would spell disaster." In response, she gave a loud meow.

I smiled.

Right then the lights seemed to take on a dimmer appearance before turning red. A loud klaxon reverberated throughout the chamber. The fish actually swam back from the front of the tanks.

Joyce raced past us with a rifle slung over her shoulders. "Take cover folks, this is not a drill."

"What's happening?" asked Mark.

"Take a look," yelled Joyce, nodding in the direction of a tunnel that led to the back of the aquarium.

In the distance I could make out the figure of what appeared to be a zombie. A light lit him up from behind, making him appear a lot like a silhouette.

Mark grabbed my elbow but before we could flee, a loud rifle shot was heard and the zombie fell.

Joyce locked up her weapon. "I'm not sure how that one got in."

For now Mark and I could take a break from the chaos of the world. The Aquaria was a dream come true yet I knew in my heart that soon I must find my mother, no matter what kinds of differences we may have, or what may be left of the city outside. Perhaps this understanding is what being called an adult was all about.

"Aqua, you must come and see this!"

I'd never seen that wheelchair move as fast as it did as when Mark led me to the dolphin tank.

BOOK TWO—
AQUA MARINE BIOLOGIST

The Aquaria Chronicles

CHAPTER EIGHT— ILLUMINATE

The Aquaria Chronicles

I MARVELLED AT THE MAINTENANCE REQUIRED to look after the aquariums. Each tank contained a scenario for fish. Within one, small clownfish had a small sunken pirate ship to swim through. Another tank had mermaid figurines. A third contained a replica of the Titanic. I'm sure the fish enjoyed swimming back and forth among these ruins.

I had a good look at the ceiling. The aquarium ceiling must have been composed of about sixteen tanks all connected together. I could see a faint line of invisible aluminum directly above me. This would keep certain types of fish safe from each other, so that the larger ones didn't gobble up the smaller fish.

The walls were also covered in gigantic aquariums. One side had octopi, the other had lobster and crab. I wondered if these fish were for eating, or were they purely kept for research? The wall tanks were sparkling clean. Someone spent time to look after all the tanks and kept the creatures healthy. Even the back wall contained a tank, but it was so far in the distance I couldn't see what inhabited it.

One octopus to the left of me slowly slid down the glass. The suckers on that baby were pink and gooey. I wanted to reach out and touch the suckers but of course the glass was between us.

As I gazed upwards I could see that the entire building contained five levels. Windows poked out of every level. Each apartment appeared to have small rooms. Perhaps they were the living quarters for the staff. None had any curtains so I wondered how they had any privacy at night. What was a great feature was that each window looked over the central part of this chamber. Each dwelling had a great view of at least one aquarium from at least two directions. It must be great to be on the top floor, or even the bottom floor, as you would literally be surrounded by water.

I briefly wondered how claustrophobic a person could get in here, surrounded only by glass, water, and fish.

Joyce led us forward. She knew we were fascinated by our surroundings so she gave us time to absorb it all.

I hadn't given much thought to the large tubes off to the sides of each of the walls. They were vertical and horizontal. Plus, a huge spherical tank was directly in front of me. One moment it was only filled with empty air, the next a dolphin slid down a tube from the ceiling, leaped through air, and entered the spherical tank. As he entered the tank, it filled with water. He swam in circles for a bit. Believe me, he was not cramped, he must have had a good thirty metre circumference to swim around in. When he got bored he swam out through a tube on the side. I lost sight of him as he headed along the wall.

I wanted to ask Joyce a question.

"How does he know when to enter the water tank? What if he lands on the floor?

"Dolphins have excellent navigation skills," she replied. "It just wouldn't happen."

Mark had wheeled right up to the tank. He peered eagerly in.

A second dolphin exited from above, flew through the air, gave out a screech that sounded much like a "whee", and landed in the tank below.

Mark waved at it. The dolphin swam closer to get a better look at this friendly human. He put on a little water show before finally departing the tube.

Mark was delighted so he clapped his hands. That was so cute, even a guy who was almost an adult could still act like a kid every now and then.

There was too much to look at. I was getting exhausted though. I hoped we could rest soon. Even the quick meal we'd had earlier was wearing off. I expected Mirabel needed to rest too. She had spent most of the day in the cat carrier.

We watched the fish swim around for a bit longer. They were so beautiful; all different colours of the rainbow. So many different species, types, and names. This was going to be my future career. Yes, for the first time in my life, I believed that fate had led me here, to the right place.

"We're in the right place," Mark said happily.

"Yes, we are. Hey, look at the size of that crab in the pool over there," I said.

Mark looked eagerly ahead of him.

"So Joyce, is this purely a research base, or are some of these fish for dinner too?" I asked her.

"Most are for research. The food tanks are actually kept below. We don't want people becoming attached to pets and then having to eat them afterwards."

"Good idea. I"m a vegetarian myself, but I'm sure my cat will be happy to eat plenty of fish."

"Will she ever," Joyce said. She must have been about three years older than me. She was dressed like the other staff in a blue jumpsuit, not too form fitting but a bit flattering. I was hoping they would give one to me.

"Is there a school that we can attend?" Mark asked.

Trust him to get straight down to business, I thought.

"Yes, there are many different levels. We'll fit you into the best class, and also assign each of you a job. That's after you fill out a questionnaire, however. But right now, you two should try to get acclimatized down here. You could be here for a while, and we don't want anyone to suffer any claustrophobic symptoms."

We had reached the far end of the building. We were near the big tank at the back. I walked closer to see what sea creatures lurked along the bottom. I was surprised when I didn't see anything. I looked up, down, left, and right, to no avail.

"Hey Joyce, what's in this tank?"

"That's a secret. You'll learn soon enough."

Now my interest had been piqued. I looked meaningfully at Mark. He raised his eyebrows. Our weirdness metres had just gone off, just like back at the New West City bunker with its strange happenings. However, this seemed like it may be something good, not something horrific.

I double checked to make sure that the tank did in fact contain water. Yes, it certainly did. It was a light blue colour. I wondered if dye had been added, because water in nature was normally colourless.

Joyce led us onto the elevator. It was glass on all sides. We rode straight to the top of the building. We gazed at the wonder surrounding us. We were surrounded top to bottom with aquariums. It was like we were actually living in an aquarium ourselves. Well, yes, I guess we were!

"Wait here, I'm going to find a room to assign to you two. Do you mind sharing?"

Mark looked thrilled. I had a worried expression on my face.

"Relax, I'll get you a room with two separate bedrooms," Joyce said. She raised her eyes skyward.

Mark looked faintly disappointed. I tapped his

arm. He winced in jest.

"Sorry, did I hit you too hard?" I joked.

"No, you hit like a girl! Ow! Okay that was definitely not like a girl."

"Mark, we have so much to do here."

"What do you mean?" he asked me.

"Well, for one thing, after we eat and rest up, we are going to have to ask someone in authority if there is some way we can contact our parents. I'd also like to contact my friend Heather."

"I want to take that questionnaire too," he said, "And I'd like to have a job and take some courses."

"I'm not sure we should get our hearts set on staying here for long. I love marine life, but I do have a life outside of here too. I'm supposed to go back to university next week."

"Is that even possible now? The way they were talking it may be a long time before we can go home."

"Okay, so I have to add that to my list. We also need to figure out what is happening outside." I yawned. "So much to do, so little time. I also want to explore and maybe find a marine biologist to ask a few questions."

Joyce returned. "They're just trying to figure out a room for you guys that has wheelchair access and is properly equipped."

"Great thanks," he said, not too enthused. "No view, I guess."

We wandered around the building for a bit longer.

"Stephen will give you guys the grand tour later. I'm showing you the public areas, and you are certainly free to explore them on your own."

"Are there any marine biologists on staff that I can talk to?" I asked her.

Joyce thought for a moment. "We have a few, but I don't think any have safely made it here this week. But we do have several aquarists on staff, such as Steven or Mr. Owens. They're almost as knowledgeable through experience."

Joyce suggested we return to the office to see if our rooms were ready yet. While we waited, we gazed around. This was like being in a dream. It was all a fantastic dream.

"Mark pinch me."

"I could but I'm too tired to wheel myself over there."

"I hope Mirabel is alright by the entrance. Maybe I should have brought her with me."

"I'm sure she's fine," he replied.

Joyce came back and handed us each a set of keys. "Let's go get your stuff and then I'll show you to your new room."

We gratefully followed her to the elevator and back down to the ground floor. By now my feet were really dragging. It might be time for sleep, and eating could wait until morning.

We walked down across the chamber. I'm not sure if it were more impressive from above, or below, or from the glass elevator.

We grabbed our stuff. Mirabel was none the worse for wear. I felt bad about her spending so long in her carrier, but she had slept through most of it anyway.

We followed Joyce to our rooms. By now I think both of us were too tired to speak.

"Please try both your keys. I want to make sure they are correct." We were in luck, both fit fine.

We both said our goodbyes to Joyce. She promised to collect us at nine a.m. the following morning.

"There's a cafeteria but if you can't drag yourselves down there, there are beverages and snacks in the fridge. I hope you both have a good evening."

We both thanked her and walked into the room. The main entrance was the living room. There was a small closet to the side. The big glass window that overlooked the aquarium was straight ahead. The two side walls were made of aluminum. There was the bathroom on one side, and the kitchen on the other. Two small bedrooms were located on each side of the living room.

"Good night," I said to Mark. I was shattered.

CHAPTER NINE—ORIENTATE

The Aquaria Chronicles

I DRAGGED MYSELF OUT OF BED at half past eight. I wanted to sleep in but we had an appointment at 9 am with Joyce. I quickly showered and dressed.

Mark was already waiting for me at the breakfast nook. He had a box of cereal, milk, and orange juice out. I dug in as I was starving.

After a few minutes, I spoke. "This isn't going to cut it. What else is there?"

"There's some fruit in the fridge," Mark said.

I got up. I had to feed Mirabel anyway. She was winding her way around my ankles. I opened up a tin of cat food and fed her.

I then found a container of fruit salad in the fridge. I pulled it out.

"Do you want to share?"

He nodded.

We completed our breakfast. I think we were both still a bit tired from the events of the previous day.

Joyce showed up right at nine.

"I trust you both slept well?"

We both nodded and yawned.

"Still a bit tired? Well, today will be an easy day.

I'll introduce you to a few of the staff, and show you to the cafeteria. I'll also show you how to do the questionnaire, which will help us fit you into life at an aquarium. You will both need to visit the doctor for a quick checkup too."

We both followed Joyce like zombies. Were we turning into zombies? Well, I guess a trip to the doctor would sort that one out.

As Joyce showed us around the cafeteria—it was self-serve and we didn't need money to buy food but we were expected to only take exactly what we needed—I started worrying about my family.

"Joyce, I have a few concerns."

"I thought you might."

I glanced at Mark who was marvelling over the huge vending machine in the corner.

"Hey Mark come and join us! We're going to get some questions answered."

I started by asking about our parents. "Is there any way we can contact our parents? They're in another bunker."

Joyce seemed concerned. "Which one are they in?"

"My parents and her mother are at the New West city bunker," Mark replied.

"And my best friend is at the North Vancouver one," I added.

"I see," Joyce said. "Well, unfortunately there is no direct method of communication. We are sealed off from the outside world. The best you can hope to do is wait for the all clear, and when you have a visit outside, try them on a telephone, assuming they still work."

"Do you think we will be allowed to leave and check out the bunker?" I asked her.

"Well, there has been trouble outside, so that is not advised, but I'm sure you already knew that. Until they can get the bleed infestation under control, I'm afraid we're all stuck in here. Plus, there is the new threat of it adversely affecting humans and turning them rabid."

Mark looked at me. Well, that answered one question.

"Anything else?"

"That really covered most of it for us, at least concerning the outside world."

"Well, I can keep you advised about outside communications. If I find out anything further, I'll give you a call. There is a telephone in your room, plus voice mail."

We had to both be happy with that for the moment. I'm sure our family was doing well, though not in as nice of a bunker as we were.

"Aqua!" called a friendly voice. Stephen came rushing up to me. It was my new boss and old friend from the aquarium. We hugged briefly. It was great to see someone I knew.

Joyce already knew him. It turned out that they were brother and sister. I introduced him to Mark.

Joyce added, "Stephen is one of the supervisors here. He helps keep the aquarium in tiptop shape."

"Is that why the tanks are sparkling clean?" I asked. Stephen smiled at me.

"They are fantastic. I can't even begin to imagine all the work involved," I added.

"Well, Aqua, you'll wish you had stayed at the Vancouver Aquarium. Here, it is super busy," Stephen said.

"I look forward to it. My friend Mark is also interested in marine biology. He is considering being a marine biologist when he finishes grade twelve next year."

Stephen shook Mark's hand. "That's great news. We need all the help we can get around here."

We left and Joyce took us to meet the commander of the aquarium. Apparently a team of marines kept guard and made sure that the law was upheld, both inside and outside. They held even more power now that the police forces had dissipated in the city. People could thank the bleed for a major decrease in crime.

We entered their headquarters. Joyce brought us up to Derek. He was the commander of the operation. He was tall, lean and had a buzz cut. He had the deepest darkest eyes, or so I noticed until I looked away.

He shook my hand. "Nice to meet you soldier."

"Oh. I'm not a soldier. I'll be a marine biologist in a couple years," I corrected.

He looked me up and down. "I think you could use some weight training. We'll get you on an exercise schedule. You too, young man." He indicated Mark. "You both need to get in shape, and you need to learn how to fight."

I do? I guess this was going to be one of our classes here. I wondered what he could teach Mark?

Mark started getting excited when he saw who entered the room next.

"Hello, Mr. Owens!" he called. A man came over.

"Hello, my favourite student. I'm so glad you safely made it here. Where are your parents?"

"They're at the New West City bunker down the street."

"Well, that's a shame. I'll look out for you here. Most people are nice, but there may be a zombie or two in the bunch."

"Thanks Mr. Owens," Mark said, smiling back at him, knowing he was only joking.

This was awesome. We both had found friends at the bunker.

"Say, has anyone seen a little old lady and a dog around here?" I asked, suddenly remembering them.

"That sounds like Mrs. Elmbridge and Pooky. Yes, we pulled them and others in when we did a reconnoiter a short time ago.

I breathed a sigh of relief. "Great thanks."

Derek gazed at me from across the room. He

couldn't be more than a year or two older than me, yet he was a marine commander? I looked forward to chatting with him after one of our self-defence classes. He handed the two of us our training schedule.

We left the HQ and continued on our tour.

"The next thing I'll show you is our computer room," Joyce said, continuing on with the tour natter. "This is where you can take a questionnaire that will determine how you will best fit in here. You'll be assigned a job, a work schedule and which classes to take. All courses are university-transferrable."

Really? I wonder how they swung that one.

She led us to the computer lab. Each computer was enclosed in its own private booth. It afforded some privacy but you could swing away on your chair and chat with the next person over.

She showed us how to log on to the computers and gave us our user names and passwords. After we logged in we were shown how to bring up the questionnaire.

The questionnaire ate up a good part of the rest of the day. We had a short break for lunch, but then had to return to the computer lab.

Various questions that I was asked pertained to my hobbies, my interests, what my goals were. What was listed on my resume, what would people say about me, what were my likes and dislikes. The second part of the questionnaire was actually a skill set test. Math, English, history, spatial relations, grammar; we were tested on all sorts of subjects. Generally, it listed everything that a solid skills assessment should. At the end of the quiz it said our results would be tabulated and be ready for us the following day.

Joyce said we had doctor's appointments that following day too. I think she knew we were bushed and needed another day of recovery.

"Let's call it a day," said Mark. "I'm famished. Let's head to the canteen."

I followed him to the elevator. Right ahead of me was Derek. He turned and smiled at me. There was something about him that commanded respect. He didn't seem to be the type of guy you would say was nice, like Mark. There was something a bit stand-offish about him, but he was noticeably attractive.

He said hi, but did not invite us to his table. He sat with the other marines. That was fine with me, as I couldn't help but notice that Mark frowned briefly in that direction.

Mark and I made our selections then chose a quiet spot along the side.

"How'd the test go?" he asked me.

"Pretty good. If it doesn't recommend me as a marine biologist, I'll just have to become a marine instead."

"I hope not. That's your dream job. Besides, the marine commander seems a bit young to command this entire place."

"He's not," I said disagreeing. "The best person won the job."

"Won, being the key word," Mark remarked.

I rolled my eyes. Was it possible that Mark was a bit jealous of the marine?
I suppose that should be of no surprise, but personally, Mark was better looking than the marine was. But I guess a disabled person could be jealous of a young fit man who can still walk with both legs.

Or was it because Derek had taken a slight interest in me? I wasn't that much to look at. Stringy long brown hair, brown eyes, a bit of extra padding on me.

In any event I guess it really wasn't my business to figure out what Mark was thinking. I liked Mark, and as his roommate would spend a lot of time with him, to take his mind off losing his parents.

"What are you thinking about?" Mark asked me.

"I'm thinking about my future." I sighed. "I hope the years whiz past until I am a marine biologist."

"Me too. I want to see you as a marine biologist."

"You can be one too."

"I know, but I still have to finish high school first. That's a drag."

I agreed.

"So we have these doctor's exams tomorrow. Is that when we find out if we are turning into zombies or not?" I had a sip of my apple juice.

"That's ridiculous," Mark said. "Once again your

overactive imagination gets the better of you." Mark put his fork down. He was done with his lousy mac and cheese.

"Don't laugh. It's happened to some people we saw on the way here."

"I know, but I had that asthma attack and I feel fine. I certainly am not turning into a zombie," he exclaimed.

I gazed into his eyes. "Let's see. Are there any zombies in there? Mwah ha ha!" I said cackling.

"No, there are no zombies here," he said laughing. He finished his drink. "Well, what are we going to do for the rest of the day?"

"I wouldn't mind flopping on the couch and catching up with the news."

"Oh right. Not a very happy topic at the moment. The news."

"Well, I'm hoping for a clue as to when we can leave here." I swept my arms wide.

"Really? I thought this was a paradise for you? All these fish, all the aquariums?"

"It is, but as I'll keep on saying, I really miss my Mum, and my friend Heather."

Mark sighed. "I miss my parents too."

"Okay, let's head to our room. There's a TV with our name on it. Perhaps we can learn some more information."

We placed our dishes on the rack and the garbage

in the trash. I never saw anyone actually work in here but I imagine someone must have kitchen duty at least once a day.

We headed down to our room, or at least I did anyway, admiring the aquariums along the way. One tank had dimmed lighting. When I walked past, the tank lit up. It was filled with electric eels. These sea creatures had to be the single most interesting thing ever. I must read up on why and how they can generate electricity.

We stopped for a bit and watched them. I guess this was why they kept this part of the tank dimmed, to increase the lighting effect. After a few minutes we headed back to our room.

We spent the rest of evening watching the news but didn't really learn much more about the outside. Much of it was speculation, as even the news teams were stuck underground. At least they had a method of broadcast. I guess I'd just have to wait until some means of communication was set up with the surrounding bunkers, or whenever we were allowed an outside visit.

This must be how it felt to be in prison. You had your outside day visits, you had to clean up after yourselves at the cafeteria, and you lived in tiny quarters with a roommate.

I scratched Mirabel's ears. She berated me for leaving her alone for so long. In reality, back in the normal world, I would have left her alone all day for much longer. But you couldn't reason with a cat. They were always right.

She grew tired of me and jumped up onto Mark's lap. I wonder if he ever tired of that wheelchair. I guess he could pull himself onto the couch, but didn't bother. He just wheeled himself in front of the TV.

I wondered if he needed help in his room, or in the bathroom. I hoped he managed okay. I think he'd be mighty embarrassed if a girl volunteered to help out with those things.

Mark noticed me glancing at him, so he smiled back. I'm so glad to have found him. I don't know what would have happened to him if I had not found him at the bottom of the embankment. Would he have had the strength to drag himself to his wheelchair and pull himself up?

"This TV is a big waste of time. We're not learning anything new." He started wheeling himself towards his room. "I'll think I'll turn in."

"Have a great sleep Mark. Have a lovely snuggle with Mirabel," I added, noticing that she was still on his lap.

She would probably sneak out later to snuggle with me on my bed. She'd slept every day of her life with me on my bed at night. I can't imagine that would change now.

I mused over what we would do the following day. A doctor's exam and our test results would come back.

Perhaps a class or two? I was ready for bed too. I was beat. What a crazy week it had been.

CHAPTER TEN— EQUATE

The Aquaria Chronicles

THE DOCTOR GAVE ME A CLEAN BILL of health. I left the examining room and waited outside for Derek. His exam would likely take longer, due to his handicap. I had never had a chance to ask him what had happened. I guess if he wanted me to know, he would have told me. Perhaps we weren't at that point in our friendship yet. I made a note to ask him later about it, perhaps even tomorrow.

Mark came out shortly.

"I'm healthy as a horse!" he said.

"Me too! Let's go, we have to go pick up our test results."

I strolled along beside Mark to the computer lab. Inside, we met Joyce. She held a clipboard in her hand. She handed each of us some papers.

They were considered private, so we took a spot at each desk to peruse the results.

Yes! Mine said I had a high aptitude for sciences. I read up and down but it didn't specifically say that I should become a marine biologist. But then, there'd really been no questions of that type on the test. But sciences was a good start. I checked the second sheet in the package. It gave me a list of three jobs that needed to be done around the bunker. On it were listed: aquarium maintenance, guide, and builder. I gathered that all three were related to the actual aquariums and that they didn't mean building an apartment. That was a relief. I signed the form to say that I accepted these jobs.

The final sheet gave me a list of course options that I could take. It mentioned that each course was two months long, so they didn't want me to take on more than three at a time. I checked off microbiology, marine biology and personal development, which was actually a combination of exercise and self-defence. I had no choice but to check it off as apparently it was considered mandatory.

"I'm working on the aquariums and taking micro and marine biology!" I wheeled my chair over to Mark. He looked a bemused. "What did you get?"

"Pretty much the same thing. Except that I need to finish three high school courses before I can graduate. Apparently down here, that can be done in two months."

"Hey, I did that. How do you think I already have a bachelor of science?"

"I don't think I'm in any of your courses though. I still have to take regular biology and chemistry."

"Bummer. But you're in personal development at 2 p.m.?"

He had a look.

"Yes, but I wonder what they think I can do in a

wheelchair." He looked a bit sad.

I gave him a little hug. "Well loads of things! Weight exercises, stretching, meditation, etc. I'm sure they'll keep you busy."

After we had perused our results, Joyce returned and collected our forms.

"I hope you made note of when your classes and work are today. Here's a list of our rules around the aquarium. Somehow I don't think we'll have any trouble with you two."

She gave us each a small booklet. A brief glance told me that there was to be no sexual or verbal harassment at the facility. No violence or abuse of any kind. Any complaints were taken to court, and serious offenders were tossed outside. In this day and age, that could be a more serious punishment than prison.

"Basically, the aquarium is an equal opportunity employer. We've tossed out those old Victorian values and have our new Millennial ones. Anyone who is unhappy with this must either keep their opinions to themselves, or leave the facility. Human life is as precious down here as the sea creatures."

"What's the weather like outside?" I asked her. In case you hadn't noticed yet, the bleed levels were also considered part of the weather. Just like the pollen count, the bleed levels also had their own section on the Weather Network or other weather channel websites.

"It looks pretty good out today. But we don't

recommend anyone go out just yet. The bleed patrol force has 10,000 members, and they are scouring the cities top to bottom. I heard Vancouver is doing well, they believe they have eradicated all traces of it. They are trying this new type of treatment which involves spraying the city with a gigantic sprinkler system every morning. But, you can imagine the drain on the water reservoirs."

I could too. Especially since every summer they claimed that there was a water shortage in the Vancouver area.

"That's just crazy," I replied. "Can you imagine how much water that would take?"

"Or, think about all the leaks in the buildings that need to be mended," Mark said. "It's going to be quite a mess when we return to school."

"Let's hope that not too many buildings leak," I replied.

Joyce led us to our first class of the day.

"We feel that health and fitness is of vital importance when you are stuck underground for such a long length of time. Here is your first class with Derek."

Derek came up and shook our hands in welcome. His hand was warm and didn't squeeze too tightly.

While we were waiting for everyone to choose mats, Derek smiled at me, so I smiled back.

Exercise class was pretty boring. We didn't even get to do any self-defence today. Most of it was stretching, meditation, and some aerobics. Derek was a good teacher and kept our mental energy levels up.

After class Mark and I separated into our separate courses. Microbiology, and marine biology weren't too taxing today. We had to write a paper on why we were interested in these courses, as well as collect our textbooks. It was a short day.

Courses were on the top floor, the fifth. I got on the glass elevator to go back down to my level. I could decide what to do with the rest of the day after I washed up. I gazed at the huge aquarium on the back wall. The one that was empty.

The faint blue colour was so pretty. I wonder what they did with this particular aquarium? Joyce had said she would tell us later, but then I had forgotten about that.

The water seemed to be shifting within the tank. Tiny waves were pushing gently around the glass.

I had nearly reached the ground floor. I think I saw something moving in the back of the tank. That was great, one of the sea creatures had moved in. I wondered whether it was a dolphin, maybe a beluga whale. Perhaps a porpoise or a shark? The long black blob swam closer to me. I wanted to take a closer look.

I exited the elevator and walked up to the tank. Was I allowed to touch the glass? I placed my hands on it and peered in. I wondered who cleaned the fingerprints off afterwards?

The creature swam closer to the edge of the tank. It was small, so it couldn't be a beluga whale, not even a baby beluga.

The object was in my face. It was Mark! I was taken aback! Humans were allowed to swim here? Okay, so that explained it. This was an aquarium for humans. Mark saw me and waved. Then he shot upwards towards the top of the tank. He was an excellent swimmer, likely due in part to his strong arms.

There was no way for me to get inside the tank to talk to Mark, so I waited in the hallway near the door. He wheeled himself out shortly afterwards. His hair was still wet but he was dressed.

"That was great," he said to me in greeting. "Just fantastic!"

"Wow, you're so lucky. Is that pool open to just anyone?"

"No, there is a swim schedule. Derek told me that tomorrow morning is also for swimming, so you'll get to try it then."

"Well, I'm not much for swimming, but I think I'd be willing to try it in that tank." We lingered in the hallway chatting.

"The water is incredible. I think they put something in it, a water softener. It feels so smooth slipping through it, like gravity has been nulled or something."

"Well, down here it's possible. Look what they've

done with the aquaria. There's definitely some advanced technology happening here." We started walking back to our apartment.

"Have you thought about how human lives are changing?" Mark asked me.

"What do you mean?" I asked, looking down at him.

"Well, here we are all packed into this research facility. Around the city, thousands of people are living in bunkers now, learning how to live in close quarters with other human beings. If there was anyone left living outside, they are likely dead, from either an allergic reaction to the bleed, or from an infection."

"There might still be some people living in their homes, if the bleed didn't get in."

"It's possible. I think they're finding that a lot of homes are built solidly, while others not so much."

"If the bleed gets inside a house it's going to die off pretty fast. It needs sunlight to grow."

Mark stopped his wheelchair in front of our door.

"True, but that dust can still cause trouble for a day or so. I learned in class that if there is bleed on a surface, that it dies naturally in a day or so. So, I can go home again once this is all over. I can clean that crap out of my kitchen, and not suffer any reaction."

"Well, not alone I hope. I can come over and help you out," I said, opening the door for both of us. "So, swimming is on the agenda for us tomorrow? Have you had a look through our little unit? Does it come with swimwear?"

"I don't think so," he replied. "I had to borrow my swim trunks but I'd prefer to buy my own pair later. We'll have to have a look in the shop later so we can pick something out."

"There's a shop here? Wow, shopping, the teenage girl can't be separated from her shopping," I joked.

"Yes, Mr. Owens was telling me about it. We can go there after dinner."

"How do you pay? Is there some sort of credit system?" I asked.

"Most items are free, but luxury items are paid from credit earned while working."

"Great, I hope it doesn't take long to earn a swimsuit. We haven't even started working yet," I replied.

Mark checked his schedule on the fridge. "I do believe I have my first shift at the mini aquariums tomorrow morning, after swimming."

I had a look at my schedule underneath. "Me too," I said delightedly. I guess the only time we would be separated was during our actual school work.

"So, we have personal development, and work together, but not our classes," I commented.

"Hey, we don't want to get sick of each other," Mark replied.

"Mark, I could never get sick of you," I said,

patting him on the shoulder.

"Me neither," he said. "I'd never get sick of myself, heh heh!"

I laughed.

We prepared our dinner. We had been getting tired of packaged meals. Some things just never changed with humans. But we had found a package of pasta in the cupboard and enough tomatoes and veggies to make a lovely spaghetti sauce. I even found a container of parmesan in the fridge.

We had a lovely meal followed by fruit salad. A glass of wine would have topped it all off, except I didn't know if alcohol was allowed down here. I saw NO SMOKING signs everywhere. I don't even think smoking was allowed in the personal apartments. I think an addict had to go to the doctor to get a patch or something and learn how to break their addiction. There was no other option down here.

After dinner we checked a map that Joyce had given us. We picked out the store easily. That was to be our evening entertainment, to go shopping. Just like in the real world. I couldn't wait! I wondered what sorts of things would be in the shop.

The shop was open in the evenings, just like the real world. I held open the big glass door for Mark. They sure liked their glass in this place, though they used a lot of invisible aluminum for the tanks.

The store looked much like a shop in a hotel lobby

would. It was filled with the usual junk food and soft drinks. There was a small selection of clothing. Some swimwear, t-shirts, pants and shorts, a little bit of underwear. A small amount of dishes. Some grocery items. A few knickknacks.

It was obvious which items would be free, and which would be considered luxury items. For the free items, they wouldn't let you take more than a basket of groceries or free items once a month, and it was all tabulated into the computer at the cashier. We wouldn't starve to death as there was still the cafeteria, but it would be nice to cook for ourselves on occasion.

We filled our baskets with things. It was nice to have things that we needed, instead of making do each day. They even had a shelf full of books and DVDs. I was already covered in the books area, as I had brought a few with me, and I knew that Mark had brought several too. I didn't want to waste our allowance on something we didn't really need.

"Hey, look at this," he said, waving an item in the air at me.

I walked over to have a look. It appeared to be one of those fake plastic aquariums that you fill up with water and plastic fish float around.

"That's really cute. Do you think you need it though? We're surrounded by fish."

"No, I just think it's kind of a funny item to have in the store." He placed it back on the shelf.

We both had a good laugh about it. A fake aquarium? Oh really? We could look around us at any given time and see a ton of fish. There was at least one wall in any given area of the facility that was just covered in aquarium glass and had many floating fish.

We took care of our purchases, than spent the rest of the evening sorting out everything and finding a spot for it in our new home.

I was really enjoying my life here. I briefly noted that my Mum would likely never approve.

CHAPTER ELEVEN— ACCLIMATE

The Aquaria Chronicles

I DON'T THINK I SAW ANYONE WEARING SWIM GEAR in the hallways, so I put my swimsuit on under my clothes. I wasn't that great of a swimmer, but this would be the chance to learn. After all, I had chosen a field where I may have to swim around a lot to study beluga whales and dolphins, so I'd better put in an effort to improve my skills.

Mark banged on the door. Guys could just slip into their suits, but girls had to fiddle with straps and closures and gatherings.

"Coming," I yelled.

When I opened the door, Mark looked excited beyond words. I could understand it. In the pool he was free, he had almost full mobility. That wheelchair didn't hold him back.

"Hurry up! I can't wait to get back in that pool," he said.

I'd wanted to ask him about his disability but right now was not a good time. I didn't want to go and depress him. That would not be good.

We met Derek in a small room to the left of the huge empty aquarium. Did you know that aquaria was the plural of aquarium? Aquaria was actually several aquariums put together. Most people don't know that. I could now talk about aquaria with full authority.

Derek wore these surfer dude bright yellow swim trunks with white starfish all over them.

Mark's voice brought me out of my reverie.

"Do we get to hop right in today?"

"Yes. I think you're both at about the same swimming level."

"Which is not too well," I said, filling him in.

"That's what I thought. You're both going to need to catch up with the rest of the team in order to do your jobs. I was told you were both joining aquarium maintenance. At some point you're going to have to suit up and go into the water."

"Are there any sharks here?" I asked.

"A few, and besides the electric eels, most of the creatures here are friendly."

"Why is that?" Mark asked.

"I think it's a spatial issue. It was either the whales, or the sharks."

"I'm glad there are whales," I said.

We had the chance to undress in change rooms, then met back in the main room. Derek indicated we were to follow him. We entered a small elevator at the back of the room. This one wasn't glass, so I couldn't see where we were going. We exited at the fifth floor. The tank filled one side of the room. Derek showed us to a door in the glass.

Below the door was a metal ladder, much like a

public pool would have.

When I realized that we would climb down the ladder and jump in, I said, "No way! That is kilometres down!"

Mark boasted, "Aqua, I just pushed myself from my wheelchair into the tank yesterday."

"You know, the only way to conquer a fear is desensitization," said Derek. "I'll go in first. Can you hold Mark's wheelchair so he can push himself out? Then after that, you can hop in."

I nodded in agreement. I got to go last. "That's great," I muttered.

Derek leapt from the door and jumped straight into the pool below. His body went in like a needle into fabric. He slipped down into the water. He fell steadily down, down, until we couldn't see him anymore. I wasn't sure of the dimensions of the tank, except that it was five stories high. Then I saw Derek come back up through the water. His arms were pushing him skyward. He finally reached the surface and bobbed up and down for a bit. He motioned for Mark to go next.

I went behind his wheelchair and held onto it. I wheeled it right up to the edge of the entrance of the pool.

"Ready," Mark said. He lifted his body up with his strong arms and pushed himself forward. He hurled through the air, then plummeted. He managed to twist and right his legs so that he entered the water feet first, in a straight line.

He slipped through the water to the depths below. A few seconds later he came back up. Both Derek and Mark tread water while they waited for me.

Here goes. I walked to the edge of the entrance. I could smell salty water in front of me. So, this must be a salt water tank. I pushed off with my feet and leaped into the water. I landed in the water at a slight angle, but that was okay, it wasn't too uncomfortable.

I had just managed to take a deep breath before my head fell below the water line. I slipped deep down beneath the depths. It had a been a while since I had done any diving like this. It wasn't so bad. I felt myself slow and slowly float back up. I paddled my arms so I could push myself back up at the surface. My lungs were just starting to feel full, so I slowly blew air out through my mouth, making bubbles. I think my lungs needed some practice too.

Finally, I reached the surface. I made sure I didn't slip back down again, and then when I was safely paddling, I let out my breathe, and took a deep one in.

Mark and Derek floated near me.

"That was great Aqua. For a moment there, I thought I might have to rescue you," Derek said.

"I would have been there first," Mark said competitively.

"Well, I don't have much planned for today, other than the suggestion that you swim around the tank, and get acclimatized with it. You will notice that on all four sides there are bars to hold onto, in case you need a break. The ladder is on the same side you entered. It's a bit of a drag climbing up, but that's the nature of this pool. I have a harness system to get Mark back up, which he is already familiar with. If you need help, I trust you both know the universal swimming symbol for help?

Mark demonstrated by waving his arms back and forth in the air. Yep, I knew that one.

"Great! You're further along than I thought. Let's get swimming."

At the beginning we trailed behind Derek, for wont of a better thing to do. Mark was right, the water was almost fluidic. I got a bit in my mouth and it tasted salty. It seemed easier to swim in this pool than the one at the public pools. I wondered if the salt water would keep us buoyant. I would ask Derek later.

After we had done about one lap around the vast pool, my muscles started feeling weary. I pushed myself over to the metal railing along the wall. I waved at Mark to come and join me. I didn't want him to get too tired and stuck in the middle of the water. It took him a bit longer as he could only move his arms, not his legs, but he made it.

"This is great," he said. "I hope we can do this every day." He was trying to calm down his panting.

Once I caught my breath I said, "We might have

to, if we're going to be working in here. I don't know about you, but I feel really out of shape. I could barely do one lap."

"I know, we need to get our swim fins."

"One more lap around the pool," Derek yelled at us, swimming past.

"We do have our first day of work today," Mark reminded me. After this we would need to wash and dry up, and head to the maintenance centre for our first day of work.

I left the railing to do another lap. The rest did me good. I was able to move my arms and legs again. My lungs were getting into the swing of things. I knew I would be stiff and sore tomorrow. That was not anything I was looking forward to. I was using arm and leg muscles that hadn't been used for at least a month.

I made it around the side, and around the next side, past the ladder. I was halfway around the final side, when I got a cramp in my leg. Oh great. I stopped and tread water. Work it out, work it out. That's what the swim instructor had said. I wiggled my toes, that usually did it. As I started writhing in pain, I made a mental note to take a calcium and magnesium supplement. I remembered that you were supposed to pinch yourself just above the upper lip to stop a leg cramp. And that's when I forgot that I needed that arm to tread water.

I took one last breath and then slid under the

water. I heard my name being yelled from behind me.

I was in so much pain and I tried not to take a breath as I went down. I released some air. I hadn't taken in enough oxygen on the surface.

I paddled my arms trying to get back up. The pain in my leg was releasing. I had my eyes closed so I couldn't see the others. I had to take a breath, I just had to. No, I couldn't!

I saw something black swimming towards me when I opened my eyes. Taking a breath, my lungs were going to burst if I didn't. My whole body spasmed, and shook. I expected to choke. I didn't, so I breathed in deeply. The fluid filled my nose and my mouth. I didn't need to swallow.

I was breathing the water! Was this the great secret?

I felt arms wrap themselves behind mine and pull me upwards out of the water. When we reached the surface. I coughed and choked. All the fluid came out of my lungs and nose. I pushed each side of my nostrils and blowed to get it out.

"Are you okay?" Derek asked.

"Yes, I think so," I said coughing.

"Let's get out of here. Can you swim back to the ladder?"

I nodded my head. Just, I think. We made it back to the ladder and I dragged myself up each rung to the top. I was grateful when I reached the top step and pulled myself through the doorway. I grabbed a towel.

Mark was already waiting. I gathered he had been helping Mark up with the harness when I had had problems with swimming.

Derek asked Mark, "Can you get out of the harness okay?" He nodded and turned in concern to look at me. "Are you okay Aqua? What happened out there?"

"I got a leg cramp and slipped under," I explained.

"It's my fault," Derek said. "I shouldn't have pushed you into the second lap."

"No, it's not, " I said. "You didn't know I would get a leg cramp."

Mark snapped his towel at Derek but didn't hit him.

"What the?!" Derek yelled.

"It's your fault!" Mark yelled.

"Oh please guys, I am fine. My leg cramp was already gone and I was floating up. It would have been fine." I patted Mark on the shoulder.

He calmed down a bit when I touched him.

"Really?" he said.

"Really. I just need to take some vitamins or something so it doesn't happen again."

He smiled at me, reassured that all was well.

"Mark, go and get rinsed off and dressed. I want to be sure that Aqua didn't pull a muscle in the tank."

Mark glared a bit at him, but pulled himself into his chair and wheeled away.

Derek stared at me. I wasn't sure if it was because he liked me, or he knew that I knew the tank's secret.

"I should have told you about the water," he said. He glanced away.

"The water was incredible. How could I breathe it in? Is it treated?"

"Yes, it is. But only a handful know that the water is treated. Please don't tell anyone."

"Not even Mark?"

"No, not even Mark."

"So, it must be an experiment?"

"In a way it is. But I don't want you breathing water again, is that understood?" I nodded.

"Do you know how it's done? Is there extra salt in it?"

"They put oxygen into some sort of substance and it naturally distributes itself through the water. This tank is extremely expensive to maintain though, so you won't see any animals in it any time soon, only humans."

I nodded in understanding.

"Tomorrow, we'll swim in the regular pool," he announced.

"Mark will be disappointed," I said.

He nodded.

I went to get rinsed, dried, and dressed. Mark was waiting for me. We'd go to the maintenance room together for the first day of our new jobs.

CHAPTER TWELVE— POPULATE

The Aquaria Chronicles

WE WERE SEATED IN A SMALL CONFERENCE ROOM, being filled in on our new jobs. Mr. Owens was the one in charge of recruitment. Mark already knew him from high school. We could be thankful for him, as otherwise, Mark would never have known to bring us here, and we could still be wandering around outside in the bleed, coughing and choking to death on blood. Our parents may have never known what had happened to us.

Mr. Owens filled us in on the aquarium. Some of the other staff sat around, and I'm sure they were bored. They'd probably heard this speech a dozen times already.

"Good afternoon everyone. Please welcome Mark and Aqua, both from New Westminster. Mark is a student of mine from New West high school. Aqua is a friend he met on the way here."

"Hello Mark and Aqua," everyone said.

I waved. This was a bit uncomfortable. I hope I didn't have to give a speech. But at least everyone was friendly.

Mr. Owens started with the tanks. "An aquarium is the singular word for one tank, either fresh water or salt water. Aquaria is the plural word, though aquariums is commonly used nowadays. Aqua is Latin for water, with 'a' as the connective and 'rium' as a place relating to water, in this case. Aquariums are commonly built of glass or acrylic, and held together with silicone, with plastic plates attached for decoration. In the past year a new discovery was made, so now we have invisible aluminum, which is a great component for aquariums. As you can see around you, several feet of thickness is no longer required for the massive tanks that we have within the research centre. Aluminum is such a strong material that the aquariums don't need to be so thick."

He took a breath before continuing. "Of primary concern to a fish minder is keeping the waste products under control. Fish, just like humans, emit waste after eating fuel. Fish, invertebrates, fungi, and some bacteria excrete nitrogen waste in the form of ammonia—which converts to ammonium in acidic water—and must then pass through its nitrogen cycle. Ammonia is also produced through the decomposition of plant and animal matter, including faecal matter and other byproducts. Nitrogen waste products become toxic to fish and other aquarium inhabitants at high concentrations. Your job will be to keep these aquariums clean, to maintain a healthy environment for the fish."

In the back of the room a young girl of about twelve raised her hand.

"Yes, Lisa?"

"Do we have to wear diving suits when cleaning the larger aquaria?"

"Yes, you will, but those lessons won't come for the newbies for several months yet, particularly for this group."

Mr. Owens stood up. Now, if you'll come with me, we'll go up to the attic, and I'll show you the cichlids. I like to affectionately call them the chicklets, like the gum."

Everyone filed out. There must have been about ten of us. It was very interesting. I hung back with Mark, as he wasn't as speedy as the rest of us.

"How are you doing?" he asked. "Any trouble with the leg?"

"It's a bit stiff. I really hate leg cramps." I massaged the side of my calf muscle.

"I guess we won't be allowed to go in by ourselves any time soon."

I motioned him forward so we didn't fall too far behind the class.

"Definitely not." I answered.

This second part of the class involved Mr. Owens pulling out a little squeegee. He showed us how to don rubber gloves, then reach down into the tanks and clean the sides of the glass. There were several attachments to add length. These tanks comprised the ceiling of the entire facility. They were about four feet tall, and I think I mentioned that the ceiling consisted of several tanks, not one big one, in order to give each type of fish a good home.

We were each assigned a tank to clean. I had the cichlids tanks, full of beautiful blue angelfish. They looked so wispy and gossamer. Truly beautiful. Cichlids fed on the algae in the water, plus whatever fish food was tossed in. It was important to maintain the proper pH balance in the water so the fish did not die.

"Wow, you have the best tank," Mark commented.

"I know! I can't believe how beautiful they are. I think I could watch them for hours. I think this variety is on the endangered species list." I could have stayed there all day squeegeeing and scooping, but we had to move on.

The teacher took us down to the tanks that held the electric eels. Here the lighting was subdued, so we could see when they gave off their electrical charges.

Mr. Owens continued his lecture.

"Despite being called an eel, it actually is not, it's actually a knifefish, which is related to the catfish family. Its genus and species is Electrophorus Electricus, the only species under the genus Electrophorus. Keeping electric eels in captivity is difficult, and mostly limited to zoos and aquariums, although a few hobbyists have kept them as pets. An electric eel requires an aquarium of at least 200 gallons. It generally must be kept in the tank by itself, although adult electric eels generally tolerate one another. Young electric eels will often fight if placed in the same aquarium, so they have to be segregated from birth. Electric eels cannot be kept with any other fish as they will attack them."

I ventured closer to the tank to have a closer look. The eel swam closer, perhaps I was his prey?

"You will eventually be responsible for these tanks, but not today."

"Would we die if we were zapped by an electric eel?" Mark asked.

"Most likely," Mr. Owens replied. "There are three pairs of organs located inside the eel's abdomen that produce electricity. They are the main organ, what is called a Hunter's organ, and a Sach's organ. These organs comprise nearly four-fifths of their body. This is what gives the electric eel the power to generate electricity. The eel is capable of a low voltage charge, and a high voltage charge."

We all looked in amazement at each other. Eels had built in power switches!

"The eel will use its electric charge to zap its prey to death."

I shuddered.

We were allowed to clean the outsides of the tanks. I had my answer from the day before about who cleans the fingerprints off the tanks. Apparently it was me.

We finished up our work and then it was dinner time again. Mark and I agreed to not eat in the cafeteria. We could cook up better meals in our apartment. The food in the cafeteria was mostly junk food and I didn't think it was too healthy.

We prepared our meal and sat at the small dining set that was contained within the living room area. The table couldn't have been more than half a metre wide, and the set only consisted of two chairs. The table only held two place settings and a small vase.

"Good sauce," I said to Mark, regarding the fettuccine noodle sauce.

"My Mum always said the secret ingredient is nutmeg."   "Well, it certainly adds that extra touch."

Well, now I think was the time for me to ask a sensitive question. I didn't want to anger Mark, nor did I wish to upset him. On the other hand, if I didn't ask him, he may think that I didn't care about him either, which was not true, I cared a lot about him.

"I have a question to ask you Mark."

"Okay," he said. "Fire away." He looked up eagerly.

"I was wondering how you ended up in a wheelchair. You are in one forever right? Your back injury is permanent?"

He seemed a bit disappointed by the question. I knew it! I hope I wasn't being overly sensitive. Well, it was too late now.

"It's from the usual. A bad car accident. It happened when I was nine. I went to a party with my parents at a relative's house. My Dad had been drinking too much that night." He stopped.

"Oh my god! I had no idea! You can stop if you want to," I said, horrified.

"No, it's all right. It was a long time ago. Anyway, my Mum and me were in the car with him. He was drinking and driving and fell asleep. My Mum wasn't able to grab the wheel in time. We slid down an embankment and the car overturned. I hadn't been wearing a seatbelt as I was sleeping in the back. I think you know the rest. Fortunately, he hit no other cars, and no one was killed."

"I'm so sorry that happened to you Mark." I reached out to hold his hand.

He took it gratefully.

"I was furious with my Dad for about a year. Then he went to A.A. and stopped drinking. He's been sober for years now, and extremely repentant. He'd give me the world if he could," he explained.

"I don't know how you could ever forgive him for what he did to you.' I clutched his hand. "If it were me, I wouldn't be able to do it."

"My parents aren't actually together anymore. They have separate suites in my house."

"Really? Are they divorced?" I asked him.

He looked down at my hand. "Not yet. They spend a lot of their meals together, mostly for my sake I think. I do think they still care about each other, but my Dad's drinking really tore them apart, and especially having a disabled son. My Mum has never forgiven my Dad, and my Dad, well, he hasn't forgiven himself either. It doesn't matter to my Mum about how sorry he is or the great effort he put into quitting drinking, and ensuring he found a good career."

"It sounds like they both love you, which is the main thing."

"Yes," he said, smiling weakly. "Being loved is the main thing. Nothing would have been worth it without both of my parents helping me through the first three months. It was crazy, I was in so much pain, all the operations, then finding out I would never walk again. I would never have been able to do it if I had been an orphan."

"I had wanted to ask you about it sooner, but I didn't know if I should or not.

"Why not?" he asked.

"It's silly, but I thought perhaps it was none of my business or you may be sensitive about it. Maybe you thought I should already know. And you never asked me about my parents."

He looked up at me.

"Well, thanks for asking. It means a lot to me. I just assumed you came from a normal family, so I'm sorry I didn't ask either."

I smiled back. We were good then.

"I hope your parents get back together. Wouldn't

that be fantastic?"

"I don't know Aqua. Not all parents are meant to be together just because they had children together."

That made me think. I guess I didn't really understand that part, as my parents had been together until my Dad had died.

"What about your parents?" he asked me. "Are they still together? We have lots to catch up on."

"No, my Dad died when I was seven years old from prostate cancer." I removed my hand from his.

"I'm so sorry," Mark said. "At least I still have both my parents, even if they aren't officially together."

"Thanks! I appreciate that."

"How do you feel about it? Do you remember that far back?"

"Oh, I was only seven. I was devastated. My Mum couldn't get me to eat, I'd just lay in my bed crying or sleeping. Finally, she took me to look at cats at an animal shelter. That's how I adopted Mirabel. She was my angel. I came out of my depression and been surviving ever since."

Mirabel was having a nap on the couch. Mark looked over at her.

"I knew there was something special about that cat," he said. He continued. "So, how did your Mum cope? She must have been devastated to be left with a small child to look after."

"I think she was, but she hid it from me, as I had

issues. She's a registered nurse so while our finances had to be on a budget, we managed just fine that way."

We finished our dinner and tidied up. Mark was in his bedroom preparing for bed. I decided to chop up some fruit for the morning breakfast.

The next thing I knew, there was a loud crash that came from the other side of the room.

I glanced up and had a look around. What was the cat up to? I ran from behind the counter and had a look.

I heard Mark struggling in the other room with his wheelchair.

"What's happened?" he cried.

"I'm not sure, I'm having a look," I yelled.

I looked for the cat. She was on the end table where there had been a lamp and a decorative plate, but they were both lying shattered on the floor. She pulled herself up onto her two hind legs and started pawing the glass above her.

"You crazy cat, what are you looking at?"

I looked up and saw a small dolphin hovering by the end of the aquarium. He had his snout placed up against the glass.

"Hey Mark, if you can get in here you should."

"What is it?" He wheeled himself in. "Oh, that is adorable!"

Mirabel pawed at what she thought was the dolphin's snout, while the dolphin thought he was being petted.

"Well, it was, until she trashed a dish and a lamp, which are both going to have to be replaced out of my earnings."

"Oh, bad Mirabel," Mark said, admonishing her with his finger.

I think she realized she may be in hot water as she jumped down and raced for my bedroom.

"What, not going to clean up the mess?" I asked her jokingly.

"Well, back to getting ready for bed," Mark said. "Have fun cleaning up after your cat."

"Yah thanks, have a good night too," I answered sarcastically.

I found a dustpan and broom, then swept up the fragments. I deposited them in the waste basket under the sink.

This was all a cat owner's duty. Sometimes cats did crazy things, then afterwards they pretended that nothing had happened.

As I was getting ready to sleep I was glad I'd had the chat with Mark. We'd been so busy with our daily lives we hadn't had the chance to really get to know each other. It was nice to finally have time for a chat.

CHAPTER THIRTEEN— CAPTIVATE

The Aquaria Chronicles

TODAY'S EXERCISE CLASS was basic self-defence. Mark had to sit this one out, so he was off swimming with Joyce in the pool. I wanted to join him but Derek said I needed a break after my traumatic experience from the morning before.

"Now, stand like this on the floor. No, stand sideways like this." He demonstrated. "This gives a smaller field for your enemy to attack."

I still didn't get it. Derek had to turn me sideways and nudged my left knee forward. Did he just touch me?

"Now, place your left elbow up like this." His left elbow went up in the air.

I tried to follow his move.

"Next, make a fist and place your right arm behind you. This will give you plenty of momentum in the event of an attack."

"Momentum, how?"

He sighed. "For you to punch someone in the nose."

I thought violence wasn't allowed here?

"So, why would I need to know that here?" I asked.

He sighed again. He was losing patience with me. He adjusted my arms, and I could have sworn that he lingered.

"You're safe here. I meant if you go outside where there are zombies wandering around that you should be able to defend yourself. Though I expect the Special Forces have killed many of them."

"Why would I need to go out?" I playfully swung my fist forward, stopping just centimetres from his left eye.

"That's great, that's some progress. They're talking about some day trips above ground. If you're chosen, you're going to have to be able to defend yourself in the event of an attack."

"Oh right, that," I said blasé. I practiced my defence and blocked his punch with my left arm. It just glanced off. I could get the hang of this.

"We were attacked twice times, no, technically three times, while we were finding this bunker."

His face flickered with a brief note of concern, before switching to his normally serene face.

"Well, you already know how important self-defence is then."

I nodded.

"Do you want to have lunch together later? I'd say I was buying, but it's all free anyway."

"Sure, sounds great!" I smiled.

Lisa, the young girl, was practicing with a boy and

she glared at me. Like honestly, would he want to chat with a twelve year old over lunch?

He showed me a few more defence moves before I had to go to my next class.

"Meet me outside this door at noon," he said. "And don't be late."

"Sure, see you then," I said, smiling.

I headed off to my marine biology class. I actually found it a bit dull. The instructor talked about the animal kingdom and all the different classes that species fell under. She handed each of her students a large rolled up poster. We unrolled them and had a look at the more familiar classes of animals.

"Have a good look as there will be a quiz tomorrow." We all groaned. There were oodles of animals on it! How was I going to memorize it all?

Perhaps I just needed to know the classification system? Or did I just need to know the marine animals? I'd have to have a good look at it later and make some flash cards.

I headed back to the personal development room where Derek taught classes.

He was already waiting for me, tapping his watch.

"Seriously?" I said to him.

"The last girlfriend who said that to me is now dating a porpoise."

"What? Is that even legal?" I frowned at him.

He smiled at me. "Just kidding!"

I wonder. Was he kidding about the porpoise, or about being on time? Well, he was a marine, so I guess they were sticklers for time.

Another thought occurred to me as we headed to the elevator.

"Does this mean that I'm out of the running then?"

"Why? Because you were two minutes late?" He tapped his watch again.

"No! Because of the fact that you even brought the subject up.'

He waited for me to enter the elevator first, before entering. I liked that in a guy.

"I thought that Mark was your boyfriend?"

"Oh no," I said, horrified. "He's my best friend. Well, second best friend. My first is in North Van at the moment."

"I just knew that you two were shacking up." He said it so seriously I wasn't sure how to take that comment.

"Oh no. We share an apartment like roommates, but nothing more. We even have separate bedrooms."

"Oh okay," he said, looking a bit pleased.

We stopped in front of the entrance to the cafeteria. It looked busy in there. He gazed at me, not smiling, but with his usual serious face.

"You are so lovely," he said to me. "Plus, very good at self-defence."

"Yah right," I said. "You just want me to buy your lunch." We both laughed. It was good to hear him laugh. I don't think it happened too often, not like with Mark and I.

We walked up to the counter. "You may have anything you like," he said.

"Right. I'm going to order the most expensive thing on the menu." That would probably have been the pizza, if we actually had to pay for it. I grabbed a veggie slice, he grabbed a fish slice. I guess he wasn't vegetarian but if he only ate fish, I could probably deal with it. We poured our fountain drinks, grabbed a couple of bananas, and looked around us for seating.

At least three different sets of friends were motioning at us. I had Mark calling me, Joyce and Lisa were waving their arms, and Mark's friend Mr. Owens was motioning too. We ignored them all and headed way to the back. There was actually a small table with two chairs behind a pillar. This was about as private was we were going to get.

We sat down and dug in.

"I still haven't heard the story of how you ended up here," he asked me.

"Well," I said through a mouthful of pizza. "That's such a long story. It was crazy."

"Well, I have the rest of the afternoon," he said.

"I don't, I have to clean aquaria later," I replied.

"Well, hurry up then," he said in that marine way.

"Well, it started with me at work on Saturday. A little boy and his mother had an asthma attack from the bleed, and one of his parents died. My boss, Stephen, sent me home. When I got there, my Mum was not home. I finally found my cat, and we holed up overnight in our small shelter. The next day it was recommended that we get to the city bunker. I found a note from my Mum, so we headed over." I finished the last of my drink.

"Have you had enough to eat?" he asked me. I nodded. "Please continue on." He finished the last of his food.

"When I reached the bunker, they would not let me in. I left and found Mark lying on the ground. He'd been attacked by the guard at the bunker. They wouldn't let him in either. I helped him up, then when I snuck back, I heard gunshots, so we returned to his place.

"From there, we packed up some supplies, ate and took off. He knew of this bunker from his teacher, Mr. Owens, but didn't know exactly where it was.

"We travelled as fast as we could. The next attack came from an old man. He demanded our food. I knew something was wrong as he could have just broken into any house or a store at that point, as everyone was on their way to safety. I stabbed him with my knife, and we were able to get away."

Derek moved our knives away from me. I laughed.

"It took us forever to get a few blocks. Mark's

wheelchair does not go very fast, and I had to carry a cat carrier and my bag. Mark had to carry his messenger bag and a bag of food.

"We finally reached the development but weren't sure where to start. So we dumped our stuff under some boards, and we separated. Mark traversed the sidewalk, while I actually entered the building. I was nearly done when a security guard found me. I tried to hide, to no avail. He was going to attack me, but I whacked him hard with a hammer that I had found."

"I guess I'd better keep you away from hammers too." Derek joked, with a little smile on his face.

"Too funny. Anyway, Mark found me and said he had found something. We walked back to the cat and our supplies and grabbed them. Mark led me to an alley. We went down it until we found this metal machinery room. I broke open the lock with another knife that I had..."

Derek smiled and nodded his head. I do think he was enjoying my narrative from a marine's point of view!

"We headed inside and started searching for the door to the facility. We had nearly given up when we were trapped inside by that same guard who had attacked me earlier. Fortunately, I'd had the sense to lock the door on the inside. Mark was grabbing the cat and our stuff, and I had a hunch that the entrance could be around the plumbing pipes.

"I finally found the pipe that locked the door and accidentally pushed on it. It opened the outer door to this bunker. I yelled at Mark and we rushed inside. No sooner had that happened when the zombie broke through the door.

"Fortunately, by that time the marines knew we were there. There must be cameras in that area. They rushed out and killed the zombie. Then they led us here, and here I am now."

"That's great," Derek said. "I knew when I saw you that you could look after yourself."

"Thanks!"

"Do you want to leave and go for a walk? I'm feeling a bit guilty about eating junk food today." He patted his stomach.

"Sure, a walk would be lovely, but believe me, you are far from a pot belly."

We put away our dishes and left the cafeteria.

We had a stroll along the ground floor. That had to be one of the more interesting floors. The entrance to the facility was found here, as well as two emergency exits that Derek made sure I was aware of.

We stopped near the back of the facility in a small private spot between two aquariums. Of course I wondered if there was any real privacy here. The place must be covered top to bottom with cameras, with only our private quarters and the bathrooms being free from being monitored.

"I'm so glad I met you," he said.

"I'm glad I met you too," I said back. We smiled at each other.

"Tomorrow we are working on a special project. I hope you'll come and join us," he mentioned.

"Sure," I said. "What's it for?"

"It's for two objectives. One is to protect this facility in the event of an attack. The second is to find a way to defeat the bleed outside."

"I think I'm in the grown-up world. Those are two tall orders to fill," I commented.

"I know, but we're closed off from everyone else here and not sure if anyone else is actually doing anything. We can't stay locked up in this bunker forever. We're going to run out of food and the pipes could break and leave us without water. We'll need to leave to do maintenance at some point. A few seniors here need medical care beyond our expertise," Derek added.

"You're right. As much as I'd like to stay here forever, we're going to have to find a way to take back our home," I said.

"Now you're talking like a marine." He smacked his hands together.

"Well, Aqua, I'd like to continue chatting with you, but you have some aquariums to clean."

I wrinkled my nose. "Right! I hope to be of more assistance at some point."

"Try and think about what we just talked about. If

you have any ideas on either eradicating the bleed, or for protecting the facility, I'd love to hear them tomorrow."

"I'll think about it then," I said. "And you never told anyone your ideas at the meeting."

He shrugged. Funny, he seemed like he could be the bad guy type, but he actually was down to earth and quite a gentleman.

He walked me back to my work at the cichlid's aquarium on the top floor.

Mark rolled up to me. I had a look at his face.

"What's wrong with you?" I asked.

"I can't believe you ate lunch with that loser and then disappeared."

"Mark, he is not a loser, he is actually quite smart."

"He's only after one thing." He was waving his arms around furiously.

"Which is what?"

"Oh you know what!"

"This is ridiculous! I won't have this conversation with you. You sound like my Mum."

I turned and left him sitting there. I'd go and clean the electric eel tanks instead.

He didn't follow me.

Well, that was unbelievable! I can't believe he said that. Not only is it none of his business who I have lunch with, or where I go with said person, he is not my father. He is not even my boyfriend. He never even once gave any indication he wanted to be my boyfriend. We were friends, and he knew that.

Hell, we haven't even been friends for that long. Only fate threw us together. If it had been a normal day on Saturday, we likely would never have met each other. I was so mad I could barely do my job.

I hoped he wouldn't be at the meeting tomorrow. This was ridiculous. He'd better apologize later tonight. I didn't tell him who he could have lunch with. In fact, I'd be happy if he met a girl and had lunch with her. Why make such a big deal out of things?

CHAPTER FOURTEEN—FORMULATE

The Aquaria Chronicles

WE WERE SEATED around the boardroom table. Derek opened the meeting and announced the agenda. The first priority was to secure the bunker from any outside threat, and in the event of an attack, to protect it. The second concern on the agenda was to find a way to eradicate the bleed on the surface of the ground, so that we could all eventually leave and resume our normal lives.

I was seated beside Mark. He had apologized to me this morning. We both decided to forget the stupid confrontation, and to keep out of each other's personal business from now on.

I also felt happy to be part of the team that could actually eradicate the bleed. Imagine what heroes we'd be! We'd be in all the history textbooks. I was a woman and there needed to be more women in the textbooks, rather than written out.

"What we're going to do is go around the table and I want everyone to put forward one idea on how to protect this facility, and one idea on how to eradicate the bleed, no matter how ridiculous. We'll all keep quiet, without judgement, while everyone has his or her say, and then we'll open it up for discussion," Derek started.

The question started at Mr. Owens.

"Well to start I'd like to suggest that we put guards on all inner and outer exits to the facility. As for the bleed, I think we should do what Vancouver is doing and turn on all the sprinklers throughout the city."

"Thank you Mr. Owens. You're up next Lisa," Derek said.

Wow, Lisa looked very pleased to be getting attention from Derek. I remembered being a twelve-year-old girl but back then I was more concerned with reading books and going to the mall.

Lisa opened with, "Well, I think we should all carry weapons. That way we'll all be prepared for a zombie attack."

Derek nodded his head. This was actually a pretty good idea.

"As for the bleed, I think we should all take turns going outside and hosing it down," Lisa added.

Joyce was next. "I think that first we need to reinforce all doors leading into the facility. As for the bleed, I'm seconding Lisa that we need to take turns going out and hosing it down."

There was a murmur through the crowd. Hosing it down was a better option than going to twenty thousand homes and turning on their sprinkler systems.

Stephen was next. I'd barely had a chance to talk to him. There was always so much to do here. "My first suggestion is for us to recruit from outside, get more people to come and defend our facility. As for the bleed, I think we should burn it out. Does anyone know if it has spores? Why is it popping up so fast everywhere?"

"Good point Stephen. Mark you're up next."

Mark smiled at me. I smiled back encouragingly.

"First off, I think we need to build a big fence around the facility. The zombies are really stupid. By the time they figure out a way to get in, we could have shot off their heads."

Wow, Mark must have played a lot of video games in his time.

"As for the bleed, I've seen it first hand. Is there some way we can build a rain making machine?" Mark asked.

"Good one!" I said to him. He looked smug.

It was my turn next. It sounded like all the great ideas were taken.

"Aqua?" Derek asked me. I hoped I didn't sound like an idiot.

"I think we should all evacuate the bunker, and then blow up all the dams so that they flood the city."

Everyone stopped fidgeting.

"That's an interesting idea, Aqua," Stephen said to me.

"But, who would look after all the sea creatures?" Mr. Owens asked.

"Okay, folks, remember these are ideas without

judgement. Discussion comes later," Derek admonished.

The people around the room continued to put forth their ideas, but I think the first group of us had the best ones.

Once everyone had their say, it was open for discussion.

"Now that everyone has put forward their ideas, let's open it up for a discussion of said ideas. Please note that the secretary is taking minutes, so all ideas will be revisited later by the marines. This is what the marines do for a living, solve problems," said Derek.

Someone in the audience yawned. Derek could go on when he wanted to.

I spoke up. "I like the idea of some sort of city-wide sprinkler system, but I think we may run out of water before anything really happens."

"I'm going to nix that one, sorry Mr. Owens. The idea will be revisited later during our private meeting. I'm also concerned about the possibility of fire. We don't want to do more damage than has already been done. A fire could also compromise our underground facility," Derek explained.

"What about sending teams out to search for clusters of bleed?" asked Stephen.

I think everyone thought this was a great idea that could be easily implemented, right now.

"Yes, while there is the Force, I think we're going

to start that immediately. I'll have Joyce send out a message for recruits so we can get started."

The other ideas were tossed around for a bit.

"I belicve that we will add more soldiers at the inner and outer doors of all entrances and exits," Derek announced.

Most of the other ideas had to be considered, as they'd take more time and effort.

The meeting was adjourned.

Mark went to lunch with Joyce, so I didn't bother joining them.

I waited until Derek was done chatting with a random person here and there. He certainly was a good leader, and was open to listening to people.

"Aqua!" he said, pleased to see that I had waited for him. "Did you want to go for lunch?"

"Sure," I said.

We headed to the cafeteria.

"That was some idea you had."

"Oh yes?" I said.

"Blowing up the dams. Flooding the city."

"Oh, I know. I don't think there are even any dams in this city are there?"

"Nope. But this is the kind of thinking that makes you a marine."

"Really? I'm a marine?"

Yes, Aqua Marine."

"Oh you're too clever," I said. We had stopped at

the entrance.

He smacked his lips to give me an air kiss.

Well, that was a surprise. He was watching me to see how I would react.

"Why you rogue," I said. "We aren't even married. You are taking advantage of a lady."

"I know miss." He joined in on the fun. "However, I was hoping that you will say that you will be my girlfriend."

I was stunned. Did I really want a boyfriend? Wasn't I only seventeen and shouldn't I be focussed on my classes? I still wanted to be a marine biologist.

Was there any reason why I couldn't be someone's girlfriend and still do all that?

"Can I answer that question once this crisis has ended? It's all a bit much for me."

He looked a bit chagrined. "You're right. It's a bit soon. I must feed my good friend first." He led me through the door.

On the other side was a stunned looking Mark, with Joyce by his side. I just waved but he didn't say anything to me. They left together.

"Mark's going to help me with the octopi today," Joyce said on their way out.

It was mac and cheese in the cafeteria again, but at least I didn't have to make it. We were having lunch when we heard a disturbance from the hallway. Stephen came tearing through the door.

"Where's the Commander? We need him pronto!" He looked quite agitated.

Derek stood up and got his attention. He walked over to the door.

I hurriedly put our dishes and garbage away, and followed them back to HQ.

"What's happened?" asked Derek.

"Someone broke one of the aquariums on the top floor."

"Why would anyone do that? You mean on purpose?" I asked.

We got into the elevator.

"I don't see any water coming down. Where is the break?" asked Derek.

"Well, I think we're in luck," said Stephen. I believe it was broken from the attic. But that water could seep down at any time."

"We'll have to turn on the pumps up there to minimize the damage," suggested Derek.

When we got off the elevator Derek went to one of the telephones hanging on the wall to call for help. They only worked internally. Yes, I had already checked.

I followed Stephen to the broken aquarium. It appeared that the middle of one of them was shattered. All the water was pouring out over the floor.

"Be careful, it's going to get slippery. Can you go and find a bucket so we can save some of the cichlids?"

I carefully retraced my steps and headed to one of

the storage rooms.

I passed Derek who said that the pumps would be turned on in five minutes, and then we'd have to exit the room.

As I entered the closet I heard him telling Stephen that they would pump the remainder of the water from the tank.

I grabbed pails, mops, and sponges, anything that could be used.

I rushed back and Stephen and I started wading through the water to save the fish. Derek was scooping fish out of the aquarium, as once the pump was started, they stood no chance. Stephen grabbed the full pails and headed to the elevator.

"I'll take these to our spare aquarium on the fourth floor. It's going to be a bit crowded, but they'll survive."

I ran for more buckets. I think we did a pretty good job. Derek got almost all the fish scooped out of the tank. He was avoiding touching the front side. If the rest of the glass broke, five thousand gallons of water would come flooding out, likely drowning us.

We took a break. If we missed any fish, they were already dead on the ground.

A loud reverberation was heard through the room. Derek grabbed my arm, and we left. "That vibration could break the tank! Let's get out of here."

We grabbed the last of the buckets and pails and got in the elevator. We headed down to the next floor.

Stephen was waiting and grabbed the buckets from us. We followed him into the room where he poured the fish into a small six foot by six foot aquarium. They were mighty crowded in there, but at least we had saved them.

We heard the vibrating noise of the pumps from above. We looked up at the ceiling and saw the aquarium above us splinter into pieces. The water came rushing out of the tank. I moved for the elevator, but Derek grabbed my arm.

"We're safe here."

Thousands of gallons of water poured from the tank, along with several dead fish. The pumps worked quickly though, and the water was never more than two inches thick along the floor. About fifteen minutes later the tank was drained and all the water above was gone, leaving only a slightly damp floor.

"But, I thought the aquariums were built with aluminum? Why did it splinter?" I asked him.

"Not all of them are here. The ones in the attic have no bearing weight on them so they are regular tanks. The other aquaria that are built into supporting walls and shapes are the aluminum ones.

I frowned. Whoever had done this had understood the difference too.

"All right," said Derek. "Clean up starts."

About twenty of us filled the room. We scrubbed it dry with rags, tossing the dead fish into huge garbage bags. They were immediately taken to the incinerator before they stunk up the joint. What broken glass that hadn't been scooped up by the pump was carefully picked up with gloved hands.

When we were done we washed up in our apartments and met up in the cafeteria. Mark was nowhere to be seen. I didn't see Joyce either. We needed to touch base but I guess we could do that later. Most likely he was still busy with the octopi.

I was seated at the table with Stephen and Derek.

"What would have caused that?" I asked.

Stephen mulled it over. "Well, if the tank were going to shatter on its own, it would have failed at one of the seams. But instead, there was a big hole in the centre."

"Gunshot," Derek said.

"What?" both Stephen and I cried unanimously.

"That's exactly what a gunshot looks like when aimed at glass."

We mulled it over.

"Who would do something like that?" Stephen asked.

"I don't know, but this adds something extra to our plates," commented Derek.

I took a mouthful of my food.

"Where was all that water pumped to?" I asked.

"To the surface," said Derek.

Stephen looked at him. "Do you mean into the

drains?"

"Well, near them. We can't have plumbing sticking out of everywhere. All the water will eventually be drained away."

I thought about all that water above ground. Above the bunker, above our heads.

"I wonder if water also kills zombies?" I asked.

"I don't know marine, you're the biologist," replied Derek.

"Right. A student of marine life. I don't know much about humans, let alone zombies."

"Well, if you guys will excuse me, I have to figure out what I'm going to do with all these homeless fish." Stephen got up and put his things away.

Derek ran his hands through his hair.

"God, it's always something, isn't it?" said Derek.

I was sitting there mulling something over.

I sat upright, my eyes wide.

Derek thought I was choking for a moment and stood up.

"Is it possible that one of us is infected, and went crazy and attacked the tank?" I asked.

"Wow, Aqua, you amaze me. Why didn't I think of that?" He sat thinking for a moment.

"Our next step will be to send everyone to the clinic for a mandatory check-up," he announced.

"Well, I hope it isn't you."

I grimaced at him. We followed Stephen so we

could help manage his fish crisis. As we were helping to rearrange the fish in the tanks, Joyce came up to her brother.

"Someone trashed the hard drive footage from the top floor." Joyce threw her hands up in the air. "So, we have no way of checking who visited the floor earlier.

"Well, this just gets better and better," Derek said. "Now we have no way of finding out who went up to the attic and shot out the tank."

I was speechless. The sooner we each had our medical exams, the better. There could be a zombie amongst us and we'd never know it, unless they totally flipped out.

"Where is your friend Mark?" Derek asked me.

"I don't know. I saw him at lunch with Joyce, but not after that."

"Hey Joyce," I called ahead to her before she got away. "Have you seen Mark anywhere?"

"I think he went back to the apartment after we took care of the octopi. He looked kind of sad after we ran into you at lunch time."

I was puzzled at first, then remembered. He had obviously overheard my conversation with Derek at lunchtime. He knew that Derek was interested in having me as his girlfriend. I thought we were only friends, but even if he wanted me to be his girlfriend, why didn't he just say so?

CHAPTER FIFTEEN—SEGREGATE

The Aquaria Chronicles

I TOLD THE OTHERS I'd catch up with them later.

"Is everything all right?" Derek asked as I headed out the door.

"Yes, I'll be back later."

I headed back to the apartment. I needed to talk to Mark and make sure he was all right. This situation was ridiculous. We had already had this discussion.

I entered our unit. It was in chaos. There were things tossed everywhere. I went into Mark's room. He had his messenger bag and some other bag he had acquired since we moved in, wide open on the bed. He was tossing things into it, but most were landing on the floor.

"Mark, are you all right? What is happening?" I strode into the room.

"I'm moving out." He threw some socks into his bag. Well that was too readily apparent.

"What! Why?" I asked him.

"Because I can no longer handle you having a relationship with that moron."

"Moron!" I said in shock. "I don't get it. Derek is highly intelligent. He has to be to run this facility. He has nothing but consideration for others, and is worried about all of us down here."

"Does he now? He's pulling the wool over everyone's eyes. Look at that flood. How many people here carry guns?"

"That's crazy. I was with him when the aquarium cracked. And can't I make my own choices? Even if he is in it for fun, do you honestly think I'm going to settle down and get married now? I have a career ahead of me. I don't even want children."

"It's not so much the relationship part that bothers me," he said. "It's about what is unsaid."

"Unsaid? Do you mean between us?"

Mark flung a shirt at the bag. It was difficult packing when you were in a wheelchair. I went to pick it up and carefully folded it and placed it in the bag.

"No. You're like a sister to me. I care about you, but you are family."

I was relieved. I was afraid he wanted me for a girlfriend.

"I'm just so frustrated with this whole facility, and the way things are run."

"I don't get it?" I said. "I thought this place was well-run?"

"Right. Things are starting to go wrong here. Just like upstairs. I'm going to stay in another apartment until I can figure out a way to get out of here."

"I want out of here too." I threw out my arms.

Mark finally looked me in the eyes.

"Please break up with him. He's only going to cause you heartache," Mark begged.

"We're not even a couple," I explained. "I said I'd let him know after this mess is done."

"I have a very bad feeling about it all."

"Look Mark, I have bad feelings about things all the time. Most of the time, nothing bad ever happens." I picked up some other things that had fallen to the ground and helped him pack.

"I have a bad feeling about Derek," said Mark.

I shook my head. "What do you mean? Is he an alcoholic? Is he abusive? Is he really a woman?" I think I'd had enough about now. "Really, just what do you think?"

"Nothing quite like that," he said.

I dropped the rest of the clothes on the floor.

"Goodbye Mark, have a nice life."

He didn't say anything in return as I left the room.

I decided to go back to HQ and see if I could learn anything more about our apocalypse. Yes, that's definitely what had happened. The apocalypse was caused by the blue weed, causing humans to die or mutate and turn into zombies, and forcing the rest of us underground. And a few who hadn't turned yet were starting to go crazy and attack the facility.

I even had my own personal apocalypse happening here in in my life.

"What's wrong?" Derek asked as I entered the room. He could see how crestfallen I looked.

"Oh my stupid roommate has decided to move to his own place."

Derek had a large binder in his hand. "What's the problem? Isn't he old enough to be on his own?" he asked jokingly.

"I guess so. Look, I don't really want to talk about it right now." There were too many other ears in the room, most of them men. I'm sure they didn't need to hear all my boy problems.

We spent the rest of the morning going over the schedules for the guard shifts. They had decided to station guards near all the larger aquariums as well as entrances and exits.

Later that afternoon I returned to my apartment with Derek. There was no sign of Mark, he had gone. The mess he had made earlier had been cleaned up.

Mirabel rushed to the door. I guess she was lonely as she had lost one of her humans.

"What a lovely cat," Derek said, bending over to pet her.

"Thanks. I adopted her after my Dad died." I tossed my hoodie on the chair.

"I'm sorry to hear that." He kneeled down to pet her more easily. Once you started, she wouldn't let you stop.

"If I didn't have her, I probably wouldn't be here

right now."

"Really?" he said looking up.

"Yes, I got so depressed that I stopped eating. My Mum didn't know what to do with me until she got the brilliant idea of taking me to see the homeless cats.

"And I'm sure that all little girls love cats. It was a clever ploy on her part," Derek said, smiling. He stood up and sat on the couch. He patted it and I sat beside him.

"So, what happened to your Dad?" he asked me.

Okay, I was starting to get annoyed at having to tell so many people about what had happened. But then, it wasn't his fault, he was my friend, so he had a right to know.

"He died of prostate cancer when I was a kid. It happened pretty fast."

"Gosh, I'm sorry about that." Derek reached out to give me an awkward hug, and I accepted. Then we pulled back from each other.

We didn't speak for a while. He didn't make any moves at all. He seemed to respect my boundaries. I wondered if he had had girlfriends before as he obviously was a bit older than me.

He flicked the TV on with the remote control, but it was always the same sad news. There was never anything about an attempt to communicate with the other bunkers. I guess no one had thought of doing that. It appeared that Vancouver was getting back to normal. Burnaby and Surrey were doing well, and people had even moved back into their homes. I hadn't realized that so many other cities besides Vancouver and New West were affected. They didn't mention North Vancouver. I wondered how my friend Heather was faring. If we could have one of those day trips that Joyce had been talking about, I could give her a call.

"Any chance I can go up to the surface for a bit?" I asked Derek.

"I'm not certain. They're still showing New West as being in pretty rough shape."

"It's odd. I wonder why we were hit so hard? It's not like it rains less often here than in say, North Vancouver."

"And what's even odder is how the bleed got here in the first place," he said.

"Well, I have a few theories on that," I offered.

"Good."

"It's one of three things. It could have been genetically engineered, from say, blueberries. Perhaps it was meant to be some new type of vegetable, but something went wrong on the way. Maybe it was meant to be a weapon, but they lost control of it. Or, perhaps it came here on a meteoroid from outer space. It might have alien origins." I stopped to ponder further theories.

"That's clever. Are you sure you don't want to be a botanist instead?"

I shook my head. "No way."

He flicked off the TV. We had learned nothing.

"So, tomorrow can we go have a peek outside?"

"All right, can't see why not. We'll be careful of course, and I'll send you up with two or three of our finest marines." He jumped up then. "And now I have to get back to work. There are so many plans to make."

"Right. I can't even recall where I'm at in my schedule. It's been all messed up today," I said.

He stood by the door. "Tomorrow things will be back to normal. Or as normal as it can be here, anyway."

We hugged each other goodbye and he departed.

I decided I'd better turn in for the night. It had been another long eventful day. Perhaps tomorrow I could check out my house, see if I needed to do anything around there. Perhaps my Mum had been able to return home. If so, she was probably worried sick about me. I had never showed up at her bunker, and I'll bet the idiot guard wouldn't have remembered me, let alone told anyone a teenage girl with a cat had shown up and been refused entrance.

I'd also like to visit the New West bunker to see what was happening there. I kept on meaning to ask Joyce or Derek what they knew about the trouble there.

I made a mental list and got washed up for the evening, had a little snack, and then turned in for the night. As I flicked off the light, one thought passed through my mind, could I be a botanist?

BOOK THREE—AQUA MARINER

The Aquaria Chronicles

CHAPTER SIXTEEN—HESITATE

The Aquaria Chronicles

I WAS HAVING A LOVELY LITTLE SLEEP in my warm soft bed when the fire alarm went off. I pulled the covers over my head, but it didn't block out any of the sound. Mirabel was lying beside me and woke up. She started batting my face to get up, as something was wrong.

What was happening? Surely it was just a fire drill and there wasn't actually any fire?

I'd better get up and get dressed. I took my off jammies and pulled on underwear, jeans, and a t-shirt. I didn't know what the weather was like outside, so I grabbed my hoodie from the chair, and my purse from the counter.

It took some doing, but I managed to grab Mirabel and get her in the carrier. She didn't want to go in after all those hours she had spent in it the other day. She thought it was going to be another one of those days. I certainly hoped not!

When I opened the door to the hallway I saw others leaving their apartments. I followed them through the corridors to the main exit, with cat carrier in hand.

I didn't see anyone I knew around me. Perhaps

they were already outside? I decided not to turn towards HQ, as they had still not turned off the alarm yet. That meant they still hadn't figured out why it had been activated in the first place. I was certain that Derek would already be on the surface, along with Joyce, and Mark. I hoped Mark didn't need any assistance in coming out, but I'm sure he would manage.

I couldn't detect any signs of smoke anywhere, nor did I see any as I looked at at the vast aquaria surrounding me.

They had the main exit door open. I exited with the rest. We traversed the long tunnel to the machines room, ducking through the little door. Soon I was outside.

There were about four inches of water lying on the ground. Oh great, my sneakers were getting soaked. I slowly trudged through the water and headed to the other side of the street where everyone else was. People behind me splashed mud on the backs of my pants. This day was starting out well. On the side of the street with the grocery store the ground was only a little bit damp.

I saw Mark down at the bus shelter with Joyce. That's good, he's safe. I slowly turned in a circle, looking around me. I couldn't see any sign of Derek, so perhaps he was still in the building, trying to figure out what was happening. Maybe I should have stayed in the building and looked for him. I'll bet he was with his marines at the moment and probably didn't need me interfering. I guess I'd just have to wait for him to do what he had to do, and catch up to him later.

Mr. Owens and Stephen came rushing up to me. Finally, a few friendly faces. I didn't know how many people lived in the bunker, but I counted at least one hundred heads today.

Stephen asked me, "Have you see Derek anywhere?" I shook my head no.

"I haven't seen him since last night. I just woke up. Do you think he is still at HQ?" I was a bit concerned at this point as no one else had seen him either.

Stephen shook his head to the negative. "We just came from there. We assumed he was sleeping or something. There was no one in HQ at all. Most of the marines were by the exit, getting everyone through."

"Do you think it is really a fire drill?" I asked. I motioned around me.

"I don't think so. We didn't plan on it."

I briefly thought about my discussion with Derek last night about letting me come outside. I wondered if it were possible he staged this, as a way to get everyone outside and into fresh air? Or was it just a fire drill, something that was long overdue? It actually wasn't a bad idea. Other buildings had fire drills once a year. We could not be the exception. It was very important to evacuate in the event of an emergency.

But then my stomach contracted. What about all the sea creatures? The whales, the dolphins, the fish?

What about the electric eels? Was there any plan of evacuation for them? Or would they just all topple out of their tanks when they melted or shattered in the heat?

Next chance I got, I'd have to ask Derek. If we couldn't save them all, we should at least have a plan to save a few.

"Look at all this water surrounding us" Stephen said complaining. "That spill yesterday has made a big mess."

I watched as the water slowly drained down the storm drains. I guess it would eventually clear out. I think the development was a bit soaked though. The studs may have sustained some water damage. Hopefully they didn't warp and have to be torn out and replaced. I'll bet the owners will be furious when they see this mess.

"If there's really a fire, what happens to the sea creatures?" I asked Stephen.

He pondered. "I don't think there has ever been a plan. I think most of the tanks are water and airtight. Hopefully we could get a fire under control in time to save them."

"Well, when this is over, we will have to have a chat with Stephen. These animals are important, and we can't lose even one of them. Their lives are as valuable as ours," I said to him.

Mr. Owens had been chatting with Mark, but he

came back to us.

"I'm giving Derek five minutes to get out here, then I'm heading in."

"Good idea," I said. "At least I don't see any signs of fire."

Stephen was scratching his balding head. "Have a good look around you," he told me.

I thought I'd already done that? I turned my head. "I see water everywhere, what am I looking at?" I asked him.

"What is missing?"

Huh? What is missing? Besides Derek? I saw people, I saw water everywhere, and far beyond I saw bleed in people's gardens. But there was no bleed in the water.

I listened to random snippets of conversation.

"There's no bleed in this area."

"That's right. The water nicely took it out."

"Well, that's just fantastic. At least the flood wasn't for nought."

Nothing much seemed to be happening, so I made a decision.

Since I'd wanted to be outside anyway, I really wanted to swing by my house and check it out, plus see if anything was happening at the New West bunker.

Since Derek wasn't here to stop me, I decided to leave.

"I'll be back in about half an hour," I told Stephen

and Mr. Owens.

They shook their heads. "We should stay in a group," countered Stephen.

"I really need to check on my Mum, and on Mark's parents," I replied.

Stephen did nothing to stop me, so I ran over to Mark to let him know.

"Hi, how are you doing?" I asked.

He didn't reply. So, he was still being impossible.

"I'm heading off to the bunker to check on our parents. I don't know how long you guys are going to be out here, but I'll be back in about half an hour. Can you look after my cat for me?"

He nodded his acknowledgment, but he didn't say anything. He took the cat carrier and put it on his lap.

As I left I felt really hurt by the loss of my friend. We'd been through some rough times for a few days. Now he was totally rejecting my friendship over some stupid little thing. We barely even knew each other and he thought he had a right to tell me who to date or not.

I jogged down First Avenue to my house. It was on Second Street and not too far from here. I didn't see many signs of people. There were a few guys from the Forces out watering some patches of the bleed. They were all suited up and I thought I should have brought some sort of protection with me, but didn't.

As I looked around me I was shocked at the bleed infestation. Besides where there were some patches of water, it was everywhere. As I ran, I churned up some of its dust on the sidewalk.

I pulled my hoodie over my face, and put on my sunglasses. It was the best I could do. So far I had been immune to any sort of allergic reaction. I didn't know if that was a good thing or not. Perhaps those who were immune were the ones who turned into the zombies?

I reached my house in no time at all. The ground was covered in bleed, but I didn't see too much higher up.

I went to the front tap and turned on the sprinklers. Then I went around back and turned on that one too. Once the water hid the bleed, it melted away into nothing. You couldn't even see it anymore.

It was now time for me to check inside the house and see if my Mum had come home yet.

I went inside, and everything was the same as I had left it before. I checked the telephone and the answering machine, but the telephone didn't work, and the power was out, so there was no way I could check the machine.

"Hey Mum? Are you home?"

There was no sound. I walked from room to room, but she wasn't anywhere inside.

I checked the hallway. I had left the bunker doors open, but she was not in there either. Okay, so that answered that question.

It was now time for me to head out to check the

New West bunker.

I turned off the front and back taps. The yards were suitably soaked, and should be good for at least a day or so.

I locked up the house and was just walking down the sidewalk when a blow came from behind me. I was forced to the ground. My kneecaps connected with the sidewalk as I cried out.

Someone was behind me so I rolled to the right. I clutched my purse, and briefly wondered where my knife was, but remembered I had left it back at the bunker.

I managed to get up on my knees when I felt a blow across my cheekbone. I fell down again. I needed to get up or I'd be badly injured. I rolled to my right and pulled myself to a standing position as fast as possible. I swung out my purse and hit my assailant smack in front of the face.

That didn't stop him, so I hit him three more times, and then kicked him in the groin with my right knee. That's when he went down.

As he writhed on the ground, I saw that his eyes were also glowing blue. So, he was one of the zombies.

I swung my foot back and took aim straight at the back of his neck. Bone connected to bone and he howled. My foot turned numb and I hopped up and down for a bit.

The zombie was unconscious. I hightailed it out of

there.

I ran down the sidewalk and in the direction of the bunker.

As I ran, I briefly noted that his body had lain against a puddle of water on the ground, and nothing had happened. So that must mean that when bleed and human combined, the bleed was no longer susceptible to the water. Well, that was just great. We solve one problem and come up with another.

I turned the corner to the house where I had found Mark laying on the ground.

This seemed like years ago now, when I had found him that fateful moment.

Well, I didn't regret finding him. We were friends for a bit. So, he now had issues. I would have done it all over again in a heartbeat.

I hope he was getting snuggly with Joyce. She was a nice lady.

I carefully tread down the path to the tunnel. I noted that the body outside was gone. Perhaps the Forces had carried it away.

I was then forced to stop at the entrance to the tunnel. It was covered over in huge boulders and rubble. What had happened here? I paced. This did not look good. I couldn't see any way in.

I pushed against a few of the rocks. I was able to shift some of the smaller ones.

Had it happened because of an explosion?

"Hello?" I heard a voice say behind me.

I whirled around, purse at the ready.

There was a Special Forces woman standing there in her uniform. I edged closer but didn't see any signs of bleed in her eyes. She had a pistol raised at me, and was also looking at my eyes.

I edged closer to her.

"It's all right, I'm not a zombie," I said.

She put her gun away, looking relieved.

"It's still hard to tell at first sight," she said.

"My name is Aqua. My Mum is in there, and so are my friend's parents."

A sad expression came across her face.

"I'm Brianne. I have some bad news to tell you."

I become worried.

"What is it? What happened here?"

"I'm so sorry. This bunker was bombed." She nodded her head in that direction.

I fell to the ground. "What? Bombed? Why?"

"It was infiltrated by zombies early on. The military decided to take it out."

"What! Why?! There were human beings inside!" I said sobbing. My Mum had been in there! She was dead now!

"I'm not sure of all the details, and it's not something the Special Forces agreed with either. It became a bunker for zombies, apparently." She walked up to me and sat on the ground beside me.

She patted me on the back.

"If there had been any humans left alive in there, they'd likely have been dead on the first day. If they hadn't been, they would have been eaten eventually. Perhaps it is better this way."

I couldn't say another word. The grief was devastating. Now I had lost both my parents and Mark. Was Heather also dead too? Had I lost my only best friend because he hated me now? How was I even going to tell him that his parents were dead?

Brianne and I sat there for some time.

I didn't even raise my eyes when she pulled out her pistol and killed a zombie who was coming for us.

She must have asked me about six times. "Where did you come from?"

Finally, I pointed in the direction of the research facility.

"Were you staying at Aquaria?" She asked.

I nodded my head. She handed me a tissue and I wiped my eyes.

"It's not safe to be out here for very long. I'll walk you back to your bunker."

She helped me stand up.

We headed down the street. I don't think the walk was too eventful. I really wouldn't have noticed too much if it had been. Brianne had her gun, so she could protect us. Plus, she was professionally trained. Right now I couldn't defend myself against a spider bite.

CHAPTER SEVENTEEN—FATE

The Aquaria Chronicles

I WAS TRULY DEVASTATED. I had lost almost everything. My Dad had died from cancer, my Mum had died from an explosion. Or at least I could hope she died from an explosion and hadn't had her body torn apart by zombies.

I followed Brianne's red hair down Eighth Avenue. I didn't know what else to do. If we stayed out here, we'd either be either attacked by a zombie or suffocated to death on our own blood. Brianne placed a face mask over her nose and mouth, then handed me one. I complied.

We were passing the big box grocery store on our right. Soon, I would come face to face with Mark. What would I say to him? I really had no idea. Could I hide from him and let someone else do it? That seemed like a plan. Perhaps I could tell Derek and he could tell Mark for me. Yes, that sounded like a plan. Or perhaps I could even have Joyce or Mr. Owens do it for me. I'd tell them as soon as I got back. The sooner it was over with, the better.

As we came around the store we saw that there were no humans left on the street. Most of the water that had been on the ground earlier had drained away or was drying off the pavement.

"Looks like everyone has gone back inside. I'll see you to the entrance, and then I think you should have a rest." She patted me on the back.

I led her around the development to the alley as she wasn't certain where the entrance was. They had certainly kept that secret from the general population. There were two marines guarding the entrance. I recognized them from inside and they knew who I was, so it wouldn't be a problem gaining entrance.

"Well, I'll leave you here. You will be in good hands now. I really suggest that you stay under cover for now." She waved goodbye and left.

I nodded wearily and the two marines let me past them, and inside.

I walked sluggishly through the tunnel. My knee caps were still aching from the attack, and my eye was hurting too. I supposed I should find some ice packs once inside, but all I wanted to do was crash on my bed with my cat.

I supposed that I would have to find Mark first. No, wait. I think I'd just leave my cat with him, and head for my apartment. I could explain tomorrow right? I'm sure he'd understand. I just couldn't take much more right now.

I walked through the main chamber of Aquaria. I was glad, well, not really but you know what I mean, to not see anyone that I knew. Not anyone who would have asked me why I had been away for longer than half an hour. I think it had been hours ago.

I pushed open the door to my place, walked in, shutting it behind me. Where was the bed? I was exhausted, mentally and physically.

Mirabel came bounding up to me. I was happy to see her.

"Hi Mirabel! Did Mark bring you back here? That's great."

I picked her up and we walked to my bedroom and collapsed on the bed. I held her and she understood that something bad had happened. I sobbed into her fur, and she just lay there, comforting me.

Just when exactly had my mother died? When had the explosion happened? I should've asked Brianne. Now I would never know my Mum's exact death date. I didn't even have any remains to collect so I could scatter her ashes in the Rose Garden at Queen's Park, like we had done for my Dad.

It had been after my Dad's funeral. I had held the end of Mirabel's leash in my hand. We were standing in the lovely Rose Garden at Queen's Park. There were several varieties of roses surrounding us. It was the heat of summer. My cat waited at the side patiently. My Mum was looking surreptitiously around. She had pulled an urn out of the shopping bag she carried.

She had another look around, before pulling open the urn's lid.

She poured the contents of the urn in among the American Beauty plants. Some of my father's ashes caught in the petals of the roses. I watched as the individual particles of sand fell down catching on the leaves and thorns before settling on the ground.

My Mum put the urn away and took my hand.

Tears fell from my eyes. My cat had come closer and wrapped herself around my legs.

My Mum starting singing a familiar little poem, with a twist.

"Rose are red, bleed is blue, I am dead, and so are you." No, that wasn't right.

I woke to someone shaking me. I opened my eyes. It was Derek! Where had he been all this time? I smiled and sat up.

That was when I remembered about my Mum and Mark's parents. I started sobbing again.

"Aqua? Is there something wrong?" Derek asked me with great tenderness. He sat on the edge of my bed.

"I think my Mum died at the bunker!"

"Oh no, I'm so sorry. Can you explain to me what happened?" he asked.

"I ran home after the fire alarm to check on the house. My Mum hadn't made it back home yet, so I left. That's when I got attacked by a zombie, hence the bruise on my face." I tried to talk in between sobs. Derek shook a bit in anger as his eyes frowned.

"I knocked him down and got away. I made it to

the tunnel, but the entrance was gone!"

"What happened?" he asked, as he handed me a tissue for my face.

"The military forces had blown it up! I ran into a lady called Brianne and she told me the bunker was being held by zombies. They decided against reason to get rid of it, with all those innocent people inside." I stopped.

I took a deep breath.

"That is horrendous! I can't believe they'd do that!" Derek was livid.

"All those people inside are gone. And now I have to tell Mark that his parents are dead!" I started crying again.

I collapsed down on the bed, so he pulled the covers over me.

"Was that a fire drill we had?" I asked as an afterthought.

"Yes, of course," he said. "It was long overdue. I think everyone was surprised."

He left and I was out like a light shortly thereafter.

Some time later I woke up to Mirabel licking my face. I immediately remembered the events of the last day. I shook my head clear. I'll bet Mirabel hadn't been fed for hours. I was going to have to do it.

I climbed out of bed, and opened a tin of cat food for her and filled her bowl with fresh water. She dug in eagerly.

I realized that I too was getting hungry. I went into the bathroom and had a shower. I dried off, blow dried my hair and got dressed.

My nerves still felt on edge and I was still sad. Perhaps the worst was over. I was lucky to have a friend who cared about me. I tried to pull myself together. I looked in the mirror and my eyes were red and I had dark shadows under my eyes. Nothing could be helped for that.

I gave Mirabel a little scratch, and headed for the cafeteria.

My friends waved at me and gave me hugs. I gathered that Derek had filled them in on the death of my mother. They were smart enough to not offer any platitudes though. I think if I heard any I would break down crying.

I made some food selections without thinking about them too much. I at least made sure I had veggie options, what with me being vegetarian and all.

I had a look around the room, but Mark wasn't present yet. That was good, I could delay telling him the news. Unless someone else had already. In any event, I still had to speak to him, whether he wanted me to or not.

I had just finished my food when I saw him rolling into the cafeteria. He went and selected his food and sat on the side eating it.

If he had seen me, he didn't give any indication.

He didn't look upset, so I think no one had told him yet. There was some whispering amongst us. I think that Derek wanted me to give him the news as no had told Mark yet.

I waited for him to finish his meal. When he had put his things away, I wandered up to him.

"Hello Mark. Thanks for putting Mirabel back at home."

He nodded.

"I have to talk to you, but I don't think I can do it here."

"Let's head to my apartment. It's on this floor," he said.

"Really? I thought they'd have gotten you one on the ground."

"Nope, nothing left."

I trailed after his wheelchair.

"We can trade," I volunteered. He was still a bit icy, but at least he was talking to me now.

"That's okay. There's an elevator. So," he continued. "I'm curious as to what happened after you left the fire drill and went home? Was your Mum there? Was she at the bunker?"

"I guess so," I said. I followed him through the door, into his apartment.

His apartment was also exactly the same as mine, except that the large framed prints on the walls were different. It had the same furniture, appliances and paint colour.

I had a seat on the couch while he stopped his wheelchair in front of me.

"I'm really sorry Mark. When I got there, the bunker had been destroyed."

He looked at my face in mounting horror.

"Everyone who was living there had died."

"No!" he cried. "It can't be!"

"I'm so sorry." I took his hand. "I think it happened really fast. I've lost my mother too."

He put his face down into his hands and sobbed for a bit.

I just sat with him, much like Brianne had sat with me. Neither of us said anything.

Did this mean we were back to being friends again?

Mark seemed to suddenly pull himself out of his grieving. I noticed he had a glance at his watch.

He asked for tissue so I got some from the bathroom. He took it gratefully.

"I'm really sorry about our fights earlier," he said.

"That's all right. We've been under great pressure here, literally."

He smiled a bit at my bland joke.

"I'll make us something to eat for dinner. I know it's early, but that cafeteria food is lousy. We both need something more substantial."

As I prepared the food he gave me his condolences

over my mother's death. I took a break from cooking and gave him a brief hug.

"Thanks, friend," he said.

I think the subject of Derek would have to wait for now. He certainly didn't bring it up, so neither did I.

We had a lovely dinner and he had somehow gotten a bottle of Segura Viudas, so we shared the bottle of bubbly.

"We both need a bit of sustenance after losing all our parents," he said.

"That we certainly do."

We managed to polish off the entire bottle. I tidied up for the both of us.

I had just put away the last fork when we heard a loud explosion reverberate through Mark's quarters.

"Oh my god, what was that?" I cried.

Mark wheeled to the door and opened it.

"I think the facility is under attack," he said.

"From zombies?" I asked.

"No, silly. From your stupid boyfriend."

"What?" I was outraged at his words.

"He's leading this base to our downfall. I've overheard talking."

"That can't be true!" I said in outrage.

"He's the one who broke the Cichlid's aquarium. How else did he know that a gunshot had broken the glass, or been really interested in your theory about blowing up a dam to flood the city?"

I stopped to think. He did have a point. Derek had known immediately what had happened up in the attic. He knew that a bullet had taken out the side of the aquarium.

Something else I saw shocked me.

Mark got out of his wheelchair. This was without any assistance from his arms. He merely stood up.

"I know, don't look so surprised Aqua. I've been pretending for weeks, trying to get a handle on what has been happening in our city. Yes, I was in a car accident, and yes, I need a wheelchair at the end of the day, but for the most part, I can walk."

He wandered around the room a bit. This was incredible.

I didn't know whether to be happy for him, or angry for the deception.

And life kept on throwing curve balls at me. And was he no longer upset at our parents' deaths?

He scooped me up in his arms and gave me a kiss on the lips.

"There. I've been wanted to do that for some time now!"

I didn't know what to think. I was about to give him a piece of my fist for kissing me without asking when someone banged on the door. I took a step forward, but before I could go further, Mark grabbed my arm and pushed me into the closet. He slammed the door in my face.

"Mark, what are you doing?" I tried to open the door, but it was locked shut.

"Hey," I yelled, "Let me out!"

I heard the other door slam. I must be alone now. I kicked at the door hard. My knees jarred. They were still injured from the zombies. I kicked about five more times before stopping.

I felt around the closet. Perhaps there was a tool chest in here. My fingers connected with the hinges on the door.

Of course. The hinges were on the inside. There were two on the door. The one at the top was loose so I managed to push it up and out. It landed with a clang on the floor.

I grabbed it and used it to ease the remaining hinges off the door. I was out and running down the hallway in seconds.

What on earth was going on around here? I was so confused I didn't even know where to start, or who to trust. Derek couldn't be a traitor could he? I thought Derek only had the best interests of the aquarium at heart?

I decided that my best course of action was to head for HQ. They should have the answers that I was expecting. I turned and headed that way.

CHAPTER EIGHTEEN—WATERGATE

The Aquaria Chronicles

I SKIDDED TO A HALT once I was inside the marine headquarters. There was water on the floor, and I madly waved my arms trying to hold my balance.

"What's happening?" I asked. "Are we under attack?"

Stephen was there
\and he said, "Not from without, from within."

"What do you mean?" I asked.

"There was a minor explosion from one of the apartments. Nothing too serious as we have the fire contained. But it wasn't an accident, there was accelerant poured on the floor."

"Is it safe to stay here with all these attacks?" I asked.

"We're trying to decide if we should evacuate or not. At this point, it could be safer on the surface."

"Where is Derek?" I asked.

"Not sure," said Mr. Owens. "We think he may be involved. We haven't seen him for an hour or so."

Well that's just great. Mark may be right and Derek could be a traitor. But why had Mark locked me in the closet? Oh, perhaps he thought I was in cahoots with him, and that was a precautionary measure.

It appeared that everything was under control, for the time being. I decided to leave and look for Mark or Derek, whoever I came across first.

This was all so ridiculous, I should be able to take time for grieving the loss of my mother, when instead I am stuck looking for two of my friends, neither of whom was who they said they were. I really hoped that I was wrong about both of them, and that they were just doing their job. In any event, it needed to be sorted out, the sooner the better. So, where to start? I figured that Derek could be in the personal development room, so that's where I started.

He definitely wasn't there. I headed back to the centre of the chamber. From there, you could see for miles. If either of them were around, I should be able to spot them from below.

I had a good look around. I was about to give up, when I spotted something out of the corner of my eye. I walked towards the huge water tank in the back, the one saved for humans to swim in. There was something swimming in the water. Had they released a dolphin?

The object swam closer. It was human. In fact it was Derek. What on earth was he doing swimming at a time like this? I banged on the invisible aluminum, but he did not hear me. I guess he wouldn't as the tank had thick, well-insulated walls. He swam off to the left. I followed on foot to see what he was up to.

He was spending an extraordinary amount of time

underwater. But then the water was oxygenated, as I had discovered when I had nearly drowned during my swimming lesson. But I wondered if there was still a time limit? Did he have to come up eventually?

I watched him float to near the end of the tank. He hovered near the base of the aquarium. I saw him pull something out of his swim trunks.

I waved my arms hoping to catch his attention but perhaps the glass wall was mirrorized at this end. I'd noticed that some parts of the tanks were and some weren't, depending on whether they thought the humans may disturb the fish and mammals in the water.

He used his wrench to try and turn something in the floor. What was he doing? Was he trying to break the tank? I looked madly around me so I could find someone for a second opinion. Derek whacked at something but he seemed to be getting frustrated. Whatever he was doing, it didn't seem to be working. Was there any way I could talk to him? The only option was to head up to the attic and join him in the water. I was certain he wouldn't hurt me, even if he were up to no good.

If he were up to no good, perhaps I could talk him out of it.

My decision made, I headed for the elevator. As I stepped in, I saw Mark there. He was back in his wheelchair.

"I'm glad to see you," he said.

"Are you? Because back there you locked me in the closet!" I said, yelling at him.

"I'm sorry about that, but I don't know who Derek is working with. It's not just him trying to sabotage the tanks, but others too."

I noticed Joyce behind him. "And you don't think it's Joyce?"

She glared at me.

"No, she's been helping me have a look around," he said smiling up at her. "Have you seen Derek anywhere?"

"Yes, he's in the big swimming tank," I answered.

"Well, it's a fine time to swim," said Joyce. "Strange things are happening around here and he chooses to have fun instead!" She glared at me.

That did not sound like Derek at all, so he obviously was up to something.

"It appears that he was busy trying to fix something in there," I said, filling them in.

Mark raised his eyebrows.

"Fix something? Really? More like break something."

"Not really, he wasn't able to do it,' I said.

After I said that they didn't appear too concerned. They both got off at the cafeteria.

I continued on my way up in the elevator.

CHAPTER NINETEEN—ANNIHILATE

The Aquaria Chronicles

I HAD JUST GOTTEN OFF THE ELEVATOR at the attic. Instead of heading to the area with the broken aquarium, I headed down the hall to the big tank pool. There was more than one way to get there.

I reached the door to the small room that contained the change rooms, and the entrance to the pool. I pulled on the metal handle, but it was locked. That was odd. If Derek were in there, it shouldn't be locked, and was it normal for it to be locked during the day? I peered through the door but I couldn't see anyone in the main room. I peered beyond but couldn't see anything, and certainly not Derek. I had a look at the lock. What did I have on me that I could use to pick it? I felt through my pants pockets. I found a safety pin. This was exactly what I needed!

I fiddled with the tumblers inside in the lock, managed to get them all lined up in a straight line, plunged the sharp pin end as hard as I could and thumped the lock with my left fist. The lock popped open. Success! No one would ever know I had done it. This lock picking method did not leave any damage on the lock.

I heard noises coming down the hall so I slipped in

and closed the door. The door was transparent, so I hurriedly ran into one of the change rooms until the person walked past. I heard two sets of footsteps come closer. They tried the door and found it unlocked. They opened the door and walked in.

"That's odd, I could have sworn that the door was locked," said one friendly voice.

"I made sure it was locked. Someone has unlocked it. I think we need to check things out." I heard footsteps walking around the room. They checked the guys' changing room first.

"Do you see Derek in here anywhere?"

"No, but if he got out, we can track him down."

What were they talking about? They came into where I was hidden.

"Why, hello Aqua," Joyce said, entering the room.

"Hello? I thought you guys were going to get something to eat together?" I asked them. "But if you're still going, I'm getting quite famished."

Mark was not in his wheelchair, and he was sidling up closer to me.

"We decided we were full," he said.

"Really?" I asked. "But it's almost tea time."

"So, what do you think Joyce?" asked Mark. They looked at each and did something with their hands, like they were communicating in a secret code.

"I think we should just do it," Mark said. "I'm getting tired of her."

"Me too," Joyce said. She took a knife out of her belt pouch.

What was happening? Were they serious?

I moved back a bit. "What's going on? Is this a self-defence class?" I asked jokingly.

Joyce came at me with her knife.

"What's going on Mark? I thought I was your girlfriend!" Okay, that's the best I could do.

"I don't think so Aqua. You saw right through me," he said.

Joyce thrust at me with her knife. I remembered what Derek had taught me and turned sideways and put my left arm up. I tried to bat her knife away. She jabbed at me, coming closer. I backed up. I thought I was doing a good job, until the knife connected with my side. It slid in and out quickly. I went down.

I clutched my side, I was bleeding but not as badly as I thought I might have been if an artery had been hit.

"That's enough Joyce. We'll lock her in here and see if we can figure out what happened to Derek."

They both turned their backs to me. I rushed up behind Mark and kicked him hard between his legs. I guess I connected with a tender spot as he dropped to the floor.

"That's for locking me in the closet!" I screamed at him.

Joyce came at me with her knife again, but I ran back to the entrance to the pool and jumped straight in.

As I was plummeting down I was briefly grateful I was wearing light tennis shoes today. I remembered to take a deeper breath this time, and plunged under water. I came up fast again, and bobbed in the water.

Derek was swimming over to me. He had been in the water all this time.

"What happened?" he yelled above the sound of the water splashing against the sides of the glass. "You're bleeding!."

"Joyce attacked me! What are you doing swimming when the facility is under attack?" I tread water with him.

"I'm not swimming, they locked me up in here," he said explaining. His black hair was plastered down and his bangs hung in his eyes.

We looked up at the entrance. Joyce and Mark peered down at us.

"Have fun in there," Joyce yelled down, then they left. I saw Mark head down the hallway, but Joyce stayed and guarded the door.

"We need to get out of here," Derek said. "I've found a way out."

"Great! Where is the exit?" I asked.

He pointed way down below the pool, way at the bottom.

Oh great, I wasn't the best swimmer and I was going to have to swim underwater for who knew how long?

"I managed to work the grill loose. We can swim along the tunnels until we find a ladder we can climb."

"Well that's just great," I said, relishing the thought of having to breathe in the oxygenated water again.

He gave me a hug. "I know you can do it!"

We were still hugging when an explosion reverberated through the building. We looked up towards the middle of the facility and saw one of the aquariums burst open.

"There's no time to lose! They're going to blast the entire site. We need to get out of here!" yelled Derek.

We both took several deep breathes and then plunged under the water. Let's hope the tank held until we could get to the tunnels. It was like slipping through grease. Too bad I wouldn't have another chance of practicing my swimming in this pool. He led me down to the grate in the lower tank wall.

He pulled it off easily, as it was only hanging by a few screws. I guess he had managed to get the others loose earlier. By about now we both had to exhale all our breath and start breathing in the oxygenated fluid. Derek was used to it, but I hesitated for a few seconds. It wasn't so bad, I was doing it now! It was almost like breathing air.

As we both entered the tunnel we felt reverberations come through the water, throwing waves at us. We swam for what felt like hours. As we got further from the tank, the light faded, until we were swimming in the dark. Finally, Derek stopped.

He pulled himself up onto a metal ladder. I pulled myself up after him, feeling my way. We took a short breather. We really couldn't afford to stay much longer, as we didn't want to be trapped underground. I had a feeling that the oxygenated water was only dedicated to that one tank.

Derek gave me a big hug in the water. We couldn't really talk underground, so we just hugged.

We climbed for what seemed like hours and hours. I don't think I could have done it if I was hanging over air. The water slowly nudged me higher. I pulled one arm after the other, and used my feet to push me to a higher rung. My muscles strained and pulled. The tendons snapped painfully and I wished I could complain underwater.

We then were out of the water. I followed Derek by feel, onto a small concrete ledge. We coughed out all of the oxygenated fluid. I blew it out of my nostrils.

We were finally back to breathing real air again.

We hadn't heard much in the water, but now it was apparent what was happening inside. The explosions were consecutive.

"He tried to blame you," I said in the dark.

"I know. We had a confrontation. I was getting suspicious, as during the fire I was with you, but he was nowhere in sight. So it had to be someone that was not in the cafeteria at the time it happened. Plus, it was a bit odd that he had set fire to his own unit."

I shook my head. What utter stupidity!

The vibrations in the building were getting worse. I could barely stand up, the ground was shaking so badly.

Derek took my hand and we ran the remainder of the way. Fortunately, he knew his way in the dark. We pounded into a wall. Derek felt along it until we came to a door.

"It's locked on the other side, going out is unlocked," he explained.

We went through it and ran down another tunnel. This one had a few electric lights distributed. As we were running, a steady stream of water came after us.

We both broke onto the surface beside the condo development.

Several marines were waiting there. I saw Stephen and Mr. Owens.

"Get above ground as fast as you can! The water is coming!" screamed Stephen.

We ran down the alley, with the water lapping at our feet.

"I know where I can find a row boat," he said. We raced down the alley to the back of someone's house. Sure enough, they had a rowboat in the backyard. We set it upright, and grabbed the oars. It was a cute little red row boat. It could hold only about two or three people.

"What do we do now?" I asked Derek.

"Wait for it," he said. He nodded towards the water.

I saw water coming gradually down the alley. When it hit the boat it was four inches high.

"Oh my god," I cried. "I left Mirabel inside!" I started to get out of the boat.

"No Aqua, I'm really sorry. She's likely already dead."

I started crying.

"Aqua, please stop, you're not making it any better. There are hundreds of people trapped underground, and hundreds of sea animals. You can't cry about your cat right now."

I stopped sobbing. He was right. There was no way all those people had enough warning to get out. We had seen Mr. Owens and Stephen. But where was Lisa? Did she make it out?

By now our boat was floating in the water. We paddled down the alley.

"I suggest we get as far from the development as possible. If the bunker collapses it's going to take the whole block with it."

We paddled for about half an hour, as the water raised up higher and higher. It only stopped when we were safely in the grocery store parking lot, floating above all the cars. We had nearly reached McBride Avenue. We turned the boat around and watched the chaos before us like it was a TV show.

The marines were out floating in inflatable boats, scooping survivors out of the water. The entire development for an entire block was under water. We saw construction material debris floating along on the surface.

"I should never have given Mark my idea about flooding the city to kill the bleed," I said sadly.

"It's not your fault. If he hadn't done it one way, it would have been another, or he would have thought it up himself," said Derek.

"Look at this," I said. "The bleed is gone. There is water everywhere now."

"What a mess," Derek replied. "Even the zombies are dead." He waved at a pile of bodies in the water. We only knew they were zombies and not human as they were face up and their eyes were open, glowing blue.

"Water always wins," I murmured.

"What did you say?" Derek asked me.

"Water always wins."

"Well, you can say that again," he said, shaking water off his paddle.

"Water always wins!"

We watched as more people were rescued. I think they were lucky that about three quarters of the staff got out. Someone was carrying a clear plastic baggie of angel fish. That was something.

"Was there really this much water in the

aquarium?" I asked Mark.

"Yes, there was. There were reserve water tanks surrounding the main building, plus all the city plumbing got turned on during the explosion, and underground walls have come down, letting in the Fraser River. I don't know if this can ever been cleaned up. I'm afraid we're going to have to accept that New West City has been flooded."

I looked sadly around me.

CHAPTER TWENTY—REPARATE

The Aquaria Chronicles

DEREK AND I SAT IN THE ROWBOAT and bobbed along McBride Avenue. How things had changed over the years. One day the street is a busy thoroughfare of polluting automobiles, the next it's a river. Joking aside, we were in quite a pickle, a very large jar of pickles in fact.

Derek tried to edge closer to me.

"Can I check your injuries?" he asked me.

"I'm fine," I replied.

"That's a nasty wound in your side. You can at least let me have a look and see if I can bandage it up somehow."

"All right then." As he came closer, he was routing through the multiple pockets of his camouflage pants.

I winced as he cleaned my stab wound. What a fool I had been to even believe any of what Mark had told me. I couldn't believe he had even stabbed me in the back, literally. Derek did a good job of cleaning and binding my wound with butterfly closures. He placed gauze over the top and secured with tape.

"Try not to move around," he suggested.

"It hurts, I won't," I replied.

"We can probably find some antibiotics in one of

the houses over there, if it gets infected."

He had to move back to his side of the boat, as it was tipping a bit on my end from the extra weight.

I lay down in the bottom on the boat, gently sobbing. I missed Mirabel, and she probably had drowned in the flood. My entire family was now dead. Derek reached out his hand and held onto my hand. It was some comfort.

We let the boat carry us wherever she wanted to. We just lay there and rested. It didn't really matter at this point. Our little boat bobbed up and down. It was rather calming.

"Try to sleep," Derek suggested.

"Where's my pillow?" I joked.

I was just about to doze off when I heard the sound of a powerboat coming closer. We lifted our heads and pulled ourselves to a sitting position to check it out.

The small powerboat floated towards us. It had about three people on it.

"That bastard is coming!" Derek said loudly, then cursed again. "If I hadn't lost my gun at some point, I'd put a bullet through his head."

"Take it easy Derek. I wonder what he wants?"

The powerboat came whirring to the side of our boat. They killed the engine.

"Hello," Mark called down to us. "Do you need some assistance?"

"No Mark, I believe we've had plenty of your assistance for today," I yelled back at him. "In fact, so much assistance, that I feel a gouge in my heart."

Joyce was standing beside him on the powerboat. "Easy girl. Mark is the hero of the year. He has saved the human race from the bleed!"

One of the other guys in the boat whooped out.

"Yah right," Derek called back. "At the expense of over a thousand fish, mammals, and humans at the aquarium! That's something to be proud of. Killing helpless animals that can't help themselves! And not even giving them a chance to escape, or giving the humans a chance to figure out how to move them out of the aquarium. The bleed was nearly under control Mark. You didn't have to act without thinking. We could have made plans."

I joined in. "Yes, let's give Mark a medal for killing over a thousand people! Because, animals are people too! Let's give him a medal because he has no brains! He only thinks of blowing things up!"

"Come on, let's leave these jerks," Joyce said. She motioned to Mark to get moving.

Mark had something more to say to us before he left.

"Sorry it didn't go the way you wanted Aqua. If I could have found a better way to do it, I would have. I really would have."

"Go away," I cried. I put my hands over my eyes. I

didn't want to see or hear anything more from him. I felt a sharp stabbing pain come from my back, so I had to put my right hand back down at my side.

"One more thing Aqua," Mark called from the boat deck.

"What?" I yelled back. Couldn't I be left to grieve in peace?

He held up a cat carrier. It wasn't, was it? It was Mirabel and she was putting up a fuss and howling from within her cage.

"Mirabel, you're alive!" I called out to her.

I motioned to Derek to take it easy. I didn't want anything to go wrong.

The guys eased their power boat a big closer so Mark could pass me the cat carrier.

Mark gently eased the carrier down over the water and into my waiting arms. The boat bounced around a bit. I was careful not to put us all in the water. I slowly moved back and slipped her under the seat.

Derek looked quite pleased that she was alive too.

I reached into the carrier to pet her fur. She was a bit wet, but well and alive.

Derek proceeded to pet her through the bars, while Mark explained.

"I went back to your apartment to get her. I just couldn't leave her behind. Despite what you may think, I do have a heart. My heart breaks thinking of all the people and animals that lost their lives earlier today. My friends here think that I am a hero. Deep in my heart, I know I am not, but I have the role to play."

I didn't want to thank him, but he deserved a thank you. He seemed a bit contrite over the evil he had caused, but I wasn't going to fall for his tomfoolery anymore. But I still owed him a thank you for bringing me my cat.

"Thank you Mark. I really appreciate you saving Mirabel. You understand how much I love her and how important she has been to me in my life. Now I mean it when I say that I never ever want to see you again. You have ruined my life! Maybe one day I'll forgive you if I ever make become a marine biologist. I can't see that happening now. Oh, and I just realized that your parents didn't really die in the bunker! PS, don't ever push anyone into a closet again!"

Mark, Joyce, and their friends left in the power boat without another word.

I think Derek was puzzling over the last comment, but I think he made a mental note to ask me later about it.

Derek and I fussed over the cat. She purred happily in her carrier. It was truly unbelievable how much time she had spent in there this past week. Once we had settled in a new home I would buy her tons of chicken wire and make her the biggest cat run you have ever seen. She was going to love it!

There was a little plastic zippered pouch of treats in

a small compartment at the top of the carrier. I fed her a few through the bars of her cage. I didn't have any water, so she'd have to wait for a bit. Most cats got the majority of their water from the food they ate anyway. They were adaptable that way.

I looked around us. There were kilometres and kilometres of water. The roofs of buildings poked out of the water. A lot of debris floated around in the murk. I even saw a dead fish or two, but was trying not to notice them too much. It was going to be nasty out here in a day or so, once they started decomposing.

"Now what?" I asked Derek. I needed a place to rest. It had been a long week. It seemed like there was never any time to rest anymore.

"Shall we row somewhere?" Derek asked me. I nodded yes and pointed at some apartment buildings in the distance. We could throw a line to one of the balconies, and hop over the railing. Hopefully no one lived there anymore, so at least we'd have a dry place to stay for a day or so until we could figure out what our next step was.

We could also collect some groceries and bottled water, and probably a few medical supplies. With luck my wound would heal without much trouble. Was there a hospital anywhere near here? Likely we'd have to row our way to Vancouver if we needed one. That would be great. I looked up in the air and there were helicopters flying back and forth doing rescue operations. That was comforting. I didn't think we were in any immediate danger, so no point in waving one down.

"Will all this water eventually drain away Derek?"

"I'm not certain. It's an awful lot. It's like the flooding of New Orleans they had many years ago. I suppose the water will drain to the Fraser River. But I expect, this flood has only affected our city and not Vancouver."

"I can't believe that Mark bamboozled me. He had me thinking you were a traitor. When in fact, he was the traitor."

"I'm sure I'll forgive you," he said seriously. "Unfortunately, everyone else thinks he's a hero. Even some of the former staff of the Aquaria. I'm still in shock over what he did. It was unnecessary."

It's just not right, I thought to myself. The world was one screwed up place when the hero of the story is the asshole who kills thousands of lives, then destroys an entire city to eradicate some sort of alien plant that we know nothing about.

Let's not forget that he had locked me in the closet and lied to me too. I was so exhausted and my brain could barely even function any more. I wasn't thinking straight. The plants were our number one enemy and it appeared that they had been eradicated for once and for all.

I was so happy that the boyfriend situation had worked out the way it had. There had been something about Mark that wasn't quite right. He had been too perfect, minus the wheelchair of course. Guys who are too perfect generally turn out to be the opposite. He had a role to play in his spy game. Derek was a bit more flawed, he tried to be perfect, but he wasn't.

I realized now that it was Mark's rebel group that had been trying to break into the New West bunker. I guess they hadn't realized it had already been infiltrated by zombies. Too bad it hadn't worked out that way. Mark would have been there, and I would have never met him. They could all be living together now, in zombie heaven. I almost smiled at that idea.

I was still choked up about losing my Mum. Our last time ever together was filled with confrontation. Now all I could ever think about was that I had gone against her wishes to become a marine biologist instead. Now I would never see her change her mind and become proud of me.

In a way it was partly my fault that the Aquaria had fallen. If I hadn't found Mark in there he wouldn't have collaborated with his partners to cause the destruction of the underground bunker. It had been in my nature to help him out though. I just could not believe he portrayed a disabled person. In fact, now he made the physically challenged look bad. If I could kick him in the pants again I would.

I realized that I also had no school to go to this week, nor would I become a marine biologist any time soon. I supposed I could go back and work at the Vancouver Aquarium in downtown Vancouver. That would be about the extent of my career for the moment. Once we were out of this mess I would track Stephen down and find out what the plan was.

"What will we do tomorrow?" I asked Derek. I reached up to rub my temples. I was getting a headache. No wait, I already had a headache.

"Take a break I should think. I think we've been through way too much the past several days," he said. "Hey a trip to Hawaii would be nice."

"I think I'm seeing enough water right now that I definitely do NOT need to go to Hawaii."

"How about a trip to the Sahara Desert then?"

"Good idea," I said. "That will give us plenty of time for rest and relaxation. I don't need to do anything for oh, about one year. I guess there's still plenty of time for me to figure out how I'm going to get back to school and become a marine biologist, especially since I no longer have any parents left alive to support me."

"Yah, not sure when they'll reopen the universities, but I guess they'll have to eventually," Derek said.

We sat as close together in the rowboat as we could. I had Mirabel's cage balanced in the middle.

In the distance I saw Mark's powerboat. They were going around rescuing survivors from the water. I guess they had somewhere to take them, but I didn't want to deal with crowds of people.

"Hey look," Derek said pointing into the water.

I turned and looked. Deep down below I saw a humongous beluga whale. It was swimming back and forth among the detritus below. We watched fascinated. I hoped that it could find its way to the Fraser River from here, and then find its way back to the ocean. Perhaps it could encourage all the other sea creatures to follow.

We watched it swim towards Mark's powerboat. I held my breath.

It came up near the surface and blew air out of its top gill. The guys on the boat flipped out as they screamed and Mark slipped off the boat into the water.

I started laughing hysterically, and Derek joined in. We watched as his friends pulled him back onboard. He was fine. He deserved worse, but this would have to do for now. I do hope he thought his life was in jeopardy when the whale came for him. He deserved it. He deserved every last bit of fear that nature could serve up for him. There was such a thing as karma and it would be coming for him over and over again until he could make some sort of reparation.

After that display, the beluga slipped back beneath the water and headed southwards, towards the Fraser River. We both clapped our hands in delight.

"I have an idea for what we can do tomorrow," Derek said.

"What is it?" I asked.

"Tomorrow we can find a way to save some of the sea creatures floating through the city. We can move them from here to the sea. Then maybe in time we can rebuild our underground Aquaria again."

I smiled at the idea. I couldn't believe I'd been such a cad in even considering Mark's thought that Derek had no regard for animal life.

"Do you think you'd be up to it?" he asked.

"Definitely!" I replied. "I'd be ready to start now, but I think it's time we headed to that building over there."

As we were paddling along, a yacht drew closer to us. Imagine a yacht floating along McBride Avenue. I could. It should be renamed McBride River.

"Hello Aqua," a girl's voice called.

Oh no, not more enemies. Wait a minute, that was my best friend. It was Heather and her family on their yacht.

"We've been looking for you guys all day," Heather called down to us. "Wait, and we'll drop a ladder down to you."

I waved back at her while we waited to board. Behind her I could see that Stephen, Lisa, Mr. Owens, and a bunch of the marines and crew from the Aquaria were safely onboard.

We thought that the apocalypse that had ended our world was airborne. But as I sat in the small rowboat with my friend Derek and my cat Mirabel, surrounded for kilometres by an endless expanse of water, I couldn't help marvelling at how wrong we were.

BOOK FOUR—
BONUS SHORT STORY

The Aquaria Chronicles

THE CURE

This short story fits around Book Three—Aqua Marine Biologist, before the big climax. It offers a potential conclusion to what happened to Aqua's mother during her Aquaria Chronicles adventure. I'll leave it up to you as to whether you choose for it to be canon, or not.

~Melanie Dixon

***

AS I CLOSED THE SQUEAKY DOOR behind me, Mirabel strained against her leash, anxious to get moving. I led my furry cat on a brisk walk around Aquaria, where we lived, and I worked. Mirabel stomped down on the dirt to cover her feces, then suddenly took off across the street, yanking the handle of the leash from my hand.

I scrambled after her, panic-stricken that she may be hit by a car. Wait a minute, there were no more cars. Gasoline had long since expired over the course of six months, and the only vehicles running were those running on biofuel. She galloped down the street, with me racing after her.

I saw her one block ahead. She had halted and was sitting on the sidewalk waiting for me. Relieved, I slowed down a bit to catch my breathe.

"Hey Aqua," a male voice called to me from across

the street. I waved at Mark, my colleague from Aquaria. He was driving his wheelchair across the street towards us. I kept on walking, hoping to grab my naughty cat.

"I have you," I thought triumphantly to myself as I grabbed her leash. I then noticed a lady in tattered rags was hunched over, stroking her fur. I walked closer to greet her.

"I'm sorry. I hope my cat isn't troubling you." The eyes that gazed back at me from behind a face of craters and sores were mine. The zombie's hair colour matched mine. She was a bit taller and plumper than me. My eyes opened wide in terror. No, it couldn't be!

Mark made it over to us, his wheelchair gliding along the road.

"Aqua, I saw Mirabel take off. I'm glad you grabbed her."

Mark's eyes flew to the zombie's face, realizing the situation wasn't as harmless as it appeared to be.

"Get away from her," he cried, tugging on my hand, pulling me away, wheels squeaking in protest.

"What do I do?" I asked him, following along. Mirabel followed behind on her leash.

"What do you mean?" he asked, squinting his blue eyes.

I stopped dead in the middle of the road, trying to explain. "The face that stares back at me is my mother's!"

He dropped my hand.

"Your mother? That thing is not anyone's mother, not anymore. She used to be. She's gone. Look at her face, does she even recognize you?"

"I thought she was dead when they bombed the bunker. But she must never have reached it after all. Mirabel also recognized her," I said, explaining.

"We should kill her," Mark said, routing around in his wheelchair storage for a weapon.

"No!" I said. "She deserves a modicum of respect at least." I stomped my foot down on the ground.

"I'm going to return Mirabel to the pet shop, then we can decide what to do," Mark said.

Mirabel hopped onto Mark's lap and I followed them back. My zombie mom remained in the same spot on the street.

Over the past several months this awful weed had sprung up in New West. We called it bleed—it was a deep blue colour. It was as nasty as touching poison ivy or oak, except that when it dried out it turned into a fine dust which caused allergic reactions. It was quite toxic to asthmatics. There was also the additional problem that if a human was infected by bleed and lived, that they soon became a zombie. So, essentially in the end, they were dead a week after being infected, eaten up by hungry dogs or cats, and insect life, their bodies exposed to the elements while slowly withering away.

Mark and I had found a pet store full of animals,

and since the zombie plague had mostly died out after several weeks, albeit with most of the human population dead, we had the time to take care of them. It gave some semblance of normalcy in our world gone dead.

I watched the zombie from across the street and waited while Mark put the cat in the pet shop. As I watched, a lady dressed in a white lab coat crossed First Avenue and headed straight towards my mom.

"Hey," I yelled, "Stay away! You don't want to be bitten." I waved my hands in the air.

The woman ignored me. She dragged a cart behind her. As she neared the zombie, the zombie leaned forward and made chomping noises near the woman's neck. The woman pulled a baseball bat out of the basket and hit her over her head, brains and blood spattering everywhere.

"No," I cried. I raced across the street. I didn't want to lose my mother a second time.

The bat went back into the basket. My zombie mom tumbled to the ground. The woman bent over and hooked her arms through the zombie's armpits and pulled her up, shoving her onto the cart.

I was nearly in front of them when the woman pulled out a pistol and shot me in the chest.

Panic-stricken sounds came from behind me, squeaking wheels spinning.

"Aqua!" the sound cried.

***

I woke up slowly, events bursting forth from my brain. Zombie, mother, cat, bullet, wheelchair. I felt hungry and thirsty. I sat up quickly, my mind spinning.

The woman from the street strolled over to where I lay on an examining table. Her eyes glowed white, yet she appeared to be more human than zombie. I backed up a bit on the bed but there didn't appear to be any danger. She handed me a cup filled with some type of fluid. I drank it down quickly.

"How do you feel?" she asked.

"Better," I replied. "Why did you shoot me?" Then I remembered my mother. "Where is my mother? Is she dead?" I asked her. I gave her the cup back.

She handed me a hanky to wipe my lips. Spotted blood speckled the white linen. I touched my lips, wondering if I had injuries. Why do I not hurt? Why am not feeling anything but the warmth of the drink I had been given?

"Was that zombie your mother?" she asked me.

"Yes, it's the first time I've seen her for weeks. I thought she was dead. What is your name?"

"Samira," she told me. "I'm a doctor. There are not many humans left who haven't turned."

"Why did you murder my mom?" I asked, wiping tears from my eyes.

"There's no going back for our ancestors," she said. "But you or I, we are saved."

"What do you mean?"

"I offer a cure that essentially renders us safe from zombies, and also keeps us from completely turning into zombies."

"Why not give my mom the cure then?" I asked her.

"There's no cure for those who turned several days ago, their brains are essentially dead, their bodies decayed. Soon the insect life will finish their feasting, and their unsupported bones will fall to the ground, before turning to dust. For those of us with choices, we will live on indefinitely, rangers of the earth. She was a zombie dear, I apologize but there was no saving her, and she was of more use to me doubly dead. I needed to extract the parasite that keeps their bodies animated, to use in my vaccinations.

"You look hungry. Let me bring you some food."

As soon as she was gone I explored the room. I was in some sort of a clinic.

A sheet lay carelessly tossed over a pile of dirty linen. I pulled it off the pile. To my horror, under it lay the body of my mom. She lay dead, I mean deader than a zombie. She wouldn't be moaning and groaning down the street anymore.

There was a frantic hammering at the window. I peered out.

"Aqua!" cried my friend's voice.

Oh my God, it was Mark!

"Get me out of here! There's a crazy doctor experimenting on zombies!" I hoped he could hear me through the double-paned glass.

He nodded to the left, slipping past the window.

Samira came back into the room.

"Why did you shoot me?" I asked

"Because you were turning."

"What?" I cried. "I've been fine the past week."

"It's airborne for the bleed dear. There's no escape. Soon all humans will turn. If I can provide the cure quickly, humans can retain their faculties. Otherwise they'll turn. I wonder who is outside?" She peered out the window. "Some seek me out for the cure."

"This still does not explain why you shot me," I asked.

"To save you," she replied. "In order for the cure to work, you have to be shot by the tranquilizer dart to put you to sleep. And then, the second shot is of the vaccine. It works quickly. See." She handed a silver plated mirror to me.

"Oh my God! My eyes are glowing!"

"Yes, you are one of the new race. But the glow soon wears off, so no one will know the truth. Oh, I almost forgot. You must be starving."

She handed me a plate filled with some sort of meat. I ate it all up.

"What was that?" I asked, licking my fingers.

"Cow brains," she said.

I started retching, leaning over, grabbing the bowl from her hands so I didn't spew my vomit everywhere. And then my stomach said it wanted more.

Squeaky noises came from behind us. It was my friend, Mark.

"Hey, what is going on? I saw you shoot Aqua but besides being a bit green, she looks okay to me."

We both turned slowly, to the the sound of his voice. He held a gun in his hand, but the doctor didn't seem concerned. He wheeled himself closer.

"What the," he said as he saw my eyes.

"It's all right, I can explain," said the doctor.

"You both look like zombies but appear to have all your faculties." Mark looked us up and down.

"This is Dr. Samira," I said, introducing the both of them like we were old friends.

"Does he need the cure?" I asked.

"Not yet," she said.

"Do we want to eat humans?" I asked her.

"No, but you may get cravings for other types of raw meat."

I nodded my head, thinking a bit.

"We have a store full of people that could use the cure. Mark, Dr. Samira has been experimenting to find a cure. The best she can do is give us temporarily glowing eyes and a lifetime curse."

"Cure," the doctor said, interrupting me.

"Cure, then. I think she gives it only to people

who are starting to turn."

Mark was happy with this explanation and lowered the gun.

"Let's get back to the shop," Mark said. "I think my manager's a zombie!"

We had a good chuckle.

"If there are humans nearby, I need to examine them," Samira said.

Mark and I glanced at each other, deciding to keep the aquarium a secret for now. We didn't think the marines would take too kindly to a woman running around with a needle.

"Let's go and I'll introduce you." Mark motioned towards the door.

"Do you have enough vaccine?" I asked, glancing around.

"Sure do, it's what I've been saving for the past few months."

We headed outside and crossed the street to the shop. When we opened the door we heard screaming sounds coming from within.

Inside were several cages full of small furry animals. Mirabel was safely locked in one of them and growling at a hissing rabbit that was missing half its face. Other animals had escaped from their cages and were running around. Above us hung cages of song birds, but they were now growling rather than singing. Several guinea pigs and hamsters gave up going after the birds and turned on each other.

I ran over and separated them, placing them back in their cages.

"I sure hope you have a cure for all these zombie pets," I said to Samira.

"Oh my goodness," Samira said, recoiling in horror. She started edging towards the door. "The pets must have turned quickly."

Mark and I glanced at each other.

"What do you mean, quickly?" he asked.

"Since the last time you were here. You must have been at the clinic with me for at least an hour. When was the last time you were here?"

Mark shrugged. He grabbed the doctor's arm and led her back outside. Needing my cat fix, I grabbed Mirabel from out of her cage, taking her outside. I slammed the door shut behind us, leaving the zombie pet carnage inside.

"Samira, I think we forgot to tell you something." I set the cat on the ground.

Mark sat in his wheelchair, trying to smother a laugh.

"Well, what is it then?" Samira asked, looking a bit confused.

"The pets haven't just turned. We've been looking after zombie animals all week!" Mark and I smiled at each other, proud of what we had done.

Samira stood there with her eyes wide open.

"You're looking after zombie pets?"

"That's right," Mark said.

"There are no other humans around. We just wanted to get you to the shop to see if you could cure them too," I explained.

"Do you want to go back inside?" Mark asked. He tugged on her arm.

Samira stepped back. "Uh no, the vaccine won't work on zombie pets, sorry. Good day." She turned and ran back to her clinic.

Mark and I had a good chuckle.

"That teaches her for forcing me to take a stupid vaccine and killing my zombie mom," I said.

"I'm sorry about that," he said. "You're taking it well."

"I know. I think being a turned and cured zombie kills some of the feelings in my brain," I explained.

"Well, I can help you keep in touch with your human side," he said, holding my hand. "At least everything else still seems the same, besides the eyes," he said. "But let's hope that glow goes away before we head back to Aquaria."

"I do still care for my cat," I replied, looking down at Mirabel winding her way around my legs. "In fact, it's going to be easier for me to care for the pets as I'm no longer on their dinner menu!"

The End.

ABOUT MELANIE DIXON

MEL IS THE AUTHOR OF EIGHT BOOKS, with more on the way. She enjoyed publishing her first YA novel in the series, "The Aquaria Chronicles", in September 2016. If you love cats, please read "Just One More Purr". If you love zombies, check out Zombie Survival Club.

She has short stories published in the Confederacy of Steam Versus Zombies Anthology, as well as in Zombified: Hazardous Material, Devolution Z: October Issue, Antipodean Steam Guild Journal: Issue One, Medium, and many more.

She is known for her professionally published online content writing as Mel Dawn, with over 30,000 articles scattered over the web on any good day. Mel was a writer panelist at VCON 2014 and all Creative Ink Festivals from 2016 to 2019.

Please leave a review on Amazon and Goodreads, so that she can sell more books and write more books!

Please follow Mel on these Social Media Channels:
Official Author Website: http://melaniedawndixon.com
Goodreads: goo.gl/Od7E6Z
Facebook: https://www.facebook.com/royalcitymel
Twitter: https://twitter.com/MelDawn1
Pinterest: https://www.pinterest.com/meldawn9
Blogs: http://royalcitymel.blogspot.ca
      https://meldawn9.wordpress.com

MORE BOOKS!

Thank you for reading my book! I really appreciate it! It keeps me writing. I'd appreciate it if you left me a review on Amazon or Goodreads. It encourage more readers to buy my books when they read positive reviews.

Besides this book, you can find these other books on Amazon, in print and ebook form.

• **The Aquaria Chronicles** – full series in print and ebook
  • **Aqua Marine** – ebook only book 1
  • **Aqua Mariner** – ebook only book 2
  • **Aqua Marine Biologist** – ebook only book 3
  • **The Cure** – short story only in full series

• **Just One More Purr** – print and ebook

• **Zombie Survival Club** – print and ebook

• **Zombtown** – print and ebook coming in 2020!

• **Writing Powered Up** – Print only mini book coming in 2020!